also by
Laura Thalassa

THE BARGAINER SERIES
Rhapsodic
A Strange Hymn
The Emperor of Evening Stars
Dark Harmony

T0016914

THE Emperor OF Evening Stars

LAURA THALASSA

Bloom books

Copyright © 2021, 2023 by Laura Thalassa
Cover and internal design © 2023 by Sourcebooks
Cover design by Amanda Hudson/Faceout Studio
Cover images by cgartdesigns/Shutterstock, arigato/Shutterstock,
Studiotan/Shutterstock, Visoot Uthairam/Getty Images

Sourcebooks and the colophon are registered trademarks of
Sourcebooks. Bloom Books is a trademark of Sourcebooks.

All rights reserved. No part of this book may be reproduced in any form or by
any electronic or mechanical means including information storage and retrieval
systems—except in the case of brief quotations embodied in critical articles or
reviews—without permission in writing from its publisher, Sourcebooks.

The characters and events portrayed in this book are fictitious or
are used fictitiously. Any similarity to real persons, living or dead,
is purely coincidental and not intended by the author.

All brand names and product names used in this book are trademarks,
registered trademarks, or trade names of their respective holders.
Sourcebooks is not associated with any product or vendor in this book.

Published by Bloom Books, an imprint of Sourcebooks
P.O. Box 4410, Naperville, Illinois 60567-4410
(630) 961-3900
sourcebooks.com

Originally self-published in 2021 by Laura Thalassa.

Cataloging-in-Publication Data is on file with the Library of Congress.

Printed and bound in the United States of America.
VP 10 9 8 7 6 5 4 3

PROLOGUE
LARISSA

270 years ago

I won't be like the others.

I'm surrounded by women with sharp eyes and lying smiles. Time and experience have made them bitter. I don't blame them; I might've been this way if I had to sleep with my child's executioner over and over again. But though I pity them, I do not trust them. They would offer me up for slaughter if they knew what I intended.

I wait to flee until the night is at its deepest—until long after my husband comes for me, his gaze glinting with excitement as he pulls me from the rest of his wives and takes me to his chamber. I wait until I return, until I manage to scrub the last of his scent off my skin.

I wait while I lay my head on my pillow, the sounds the other concubines' quiet murmurings filling our chamber. I silently thank the Undying Gods that I was trained to listen rather than talk. Loose lips would surely unravel my entire plan.

Secrets are meant for one soul to keep. How many times had I whispered that into the Shadow King's ear? He thought me coy and alluring then, but soon he'll realize this entire time it was my little inside joke, and he was the fool who bought it.

I wait until every last breath in the beds around me evens out, and then I wait some more.

I wait until, eventually, the moment to act comes upon me.

I sit up in bed. Reaching a hand down the tight bodice of my nightgown, I pull out a small vial. I gave up four hundred years of my life for this thimbleful of tonic.

It was the only way.

I dig my nails under the cork and unstop it. It smells like the earth after a long rain, a smell I always associated with hope because it meant an end to the storm.

I hesitate only a moment. Then I bring the vial to my lips and down the liquid in a single swallow.

The tonic's effects don't take hold immediately, but, when they do, I smile. Ever so slowly, the hand still holding the empty glass begins to vanish. The vial slips from my grasp. I close my eyes as the rest of my clothes and the blankets that cover me suddenly pass *through* me.

Silent like the night, I slip out of bed, my exposed skin prickling in the cool chamber—though it's wrong to call what's left of me *skin*. I'm as insubstantial as a thought. I try to touch my face, but my hand passes through my cheek, the sensation of it like a phantom wind brushing against me. My stomach bottoms out.

It *worked*.

I'm incorporeal.

At last.

This is what four hundred years of life bought me.

Wish I could see the look on that bastard's face when he realizes I'm gone.

I float up from my bed, my eyes moving over my shared chambers, with all its soft sheets and softer women. I am no longer one of them.

Praise the Mother and the Father.

I drift through the window, grimacing as my body passes through the glass. The sensation isn't unpleasant, but the strangeness of it is.

I keep floating up until the city below me is nothing more than twinkling lights. From here, Somnia looks beautiful. From here, it doesn't look like the cage it became to me.

It's not until I'm some distance away that I allow myself to laugh. And once I start, I can't seem to stop.

I outmaneuvered my husband. How many times has that happened?

My eyes move to the stars, and my laughter dies. All those millions of stars, each one a tiny beacon of brightness against the oppressive night.

A wave of hope fills me.

How do you fight the darkness? You refuse to let it snuff out your light.

I let the wind carry me away, knowing it'll eventually deposit me where I need to go.

Every so often pixies flitter by me, chittering wildly. Less often, I see two sets of wings, lovers meeting high up in the night sky under the cloak of darkness.

Once I might've felt something at the sight of them—wistfulness perhaps—but now I feel nothing.

My husband stamped that notion out.

Now, as I float on the soft wind, I'm more concerned

with the single sets of wings I see every now and then. Soldiers looking for me?

I knew long before I drank the vial that I'd be leaving breadcrumbs behind—my nightclothes, the glass container itself. One whiff of it and any curious fairy would know exactly what I drank, and thus, exactly what I did.

My sick, ardent husband will do something about it. He'll have to. His pride will demand it.

I float high in the sky for what must be hours, but, at some point, I begin to drift down. I catch sight of my arm shimmering back into existence. Seconds later it solidifies, along with the rest of my body, and the drifting becomes tumbling, then falling.

An instinctive bolt of fear shoots through me. No sooner do I feel it than my wings manifest. Paper-thin, they shimmer the palest of purples. They catch the wind, slowing my descent. I continue to drop from the sky, my body seeking lower elevations where the air is thicker.

Only once I've reached a reasonable elevation do I pause.

The night air bites into my bare skin. I'm as naked as the day I was born, my waist-length hair my only covering. The ebony locks slide over my torso, swaying in the wind.

I need clothes and shelter, and I need to not be seen.

Capture at this point means certain death. Certain, *slow* death. My husband isn't known for his kindness.

My hand drifts to my stomach.

He would give me death either way.

I take a steadying breath and my eyes move to the horizon. Somewhere beyond it is Barbos, the City of Thieves. And beyond that—

Home.

PART I

IN THE BEGINNING, THERE WAS DARKNESS

CHAPTER 1
MISBEGOTTEN

257 years ago

Bastard.

Bastard. Bastard. Bastard.

It's an ugly word, one I've come to hate a great deal, mostly because I can't escape it.

I hear it whispered beneath people's breath as I pass. I see it in their eyes when they look at me. I smell it in the sour breath of the town kids who like to push me around for it. My knuckles are scabbed over from the number of times I've had to fight for my honor.

But the worst is when people use it idly.

"That Flynn boy came at my son again."

"Who?"

"You know, the scrawny bastard."

"Oh, him. Yes."

The word is only a step or two up from *slave*. And I have to wear the title like a badge of shame.

I head into the Caverns of Arestys, twisting my way through the tunnels, the flickering candle in my hand my only source of light. Not that it matters. I can see quite well in darkness, light or no.

My mood blackens as I pass through the shoddy door to our house. A bastard son living in the worst area of the poorest floating island in all the kingdom.

My mother still isn't home from her work as town scribe, so I move about our house, replacing the nubs of candles with the fresh candles I procured.

All the while, I seethe.

Every *plink* of water dripping from the cavern ceiling, every draft of chilly air that slides through the myriad of tunnels—it all mocks me.

Bastard, bastard, bastard.

I grab the beets that are laid out on the table and drop them into the cauldron in our kitchen. It's only once I pour water into the mix and then light a fire beneath the hanging pot that I actually relax enough to rub my split knuckles. Flecks of dried blood coat the skin, and I'm not sure whether it's mine or someone else's.

Bastard.

I can still hear the name, spoken like a taunt, on my way home from town.

Beneath the fresh cuts are old ones. I've had to defend my shitty title for a long time. Of course, it's not necessarily *bastard* that set me off. Sometimes it's all the insults that spawn from it.

You'll never be anything more than your whore mother. The street kid had said that to me today. His voice still rings in my ears.

It was the wrong thing to say.

The next time you say that, I warned, *you'll have a few less teeth to work with.*

He hadn't believed me then.

I slip a hand into the pocket of my trousers and touch the tiny, bloody incisors resting there.

He does now.

Behind me, the front door opens, and my mother comes in. I know without getting close to her that she smells of old parchment and her fingers are stained black with ink.

A scribe cries words and bleeds ink, she used to tell me when I was little and didn't know better. I thought it was true, that this was part of her magic. That was before I truly understood what magic was—and what it wasn't.

"Desmond," she says, flashing me an exhausted smile, "I missed you."

I nod tersely, not trusting myself to speak.

"Did you do your reading?" she asks.

We might be the poorest fairies to exist in this godsless world, but Larissa Flynn has always spent what little hard-earned money she makes on books. Books about kingdoms I'll never see and people I'll never meet. Books about languages I'll never speak and customs I'll never endure. Books about lives I want but will never live.

And under her roof I'm to learn everything within their pages.

"What's the point?" I ask, refusing to admit that I did in fact do the reading because I can't help but return to those damned books day after day, determined to change my life. Our lives.

My mother's eyes move to the candles.

"*Desmond.*" Her voice drops low as she gently chastises

me. "Who did you swindle this time?" She gives me her no-nonsense look, but her eyes twinkle mischievously.

As much as she pretends to disapprove of deals I strike, she subtly encourages them. And on any other day, I might say something to butter her up even more. Because most days I enjoy helping her.

"Does it matter?" I say, pausing over the small cauldron I'm stirring. I smell like beets and my clothes are stained a reddish-purple where the juice has splattered onto me. I gave up a decent meal to trade for those candles. Hence, beets for dinner.

I should be thankful. It could always be worse. There are nights I go to bed with a full mind but an empty belly. And in the morning, I wake up with sand in my eyes and between my toes, like I'm the Sandman's favorite damned person, and the whole nightmare starts over again.

I hate poverty. I hate feeling like we're only entitled to the worst this realm has to offer simply *because*. But more than anything, I hate having to make hard choices. Books or food? To learn or to eat?

"This wouldn't even be an issue if you would just let me use a bit of magic," I say.

I can feel my power burning under my skin and beneath my fingertips, waiting for me to call it forth.

"No magic."

"Mom, everyone thinks we're weak." The strongest fairies wield the most magic—the weakest, the least. Everyone who's met me believes I'm one of those poor, rare souls born without it entirely.

A fatherless, *powerless* fairy. Aside from slaves, this might be the worst fate for a person living within these realms.

The rub of it all is that I have plenty of magic, and now,

so close to puberty, I can feel it like a storm beneath my veins. It's taking increasing effort just to *leash* it.

"No magic," she repeats, setting her satchel next to our rickety table before taking over the stirring from me.

"So I'm to have powers but never use them?" I say heatedly. This is an old, scarred battle of ours. "And I'm to read but never speak of my knowledge?"

She reaches for my hand and runs her thumb over my knuckles. "And you are to have strength without abusing it," she adds. "Yes, my son. Be humble. Speak, but listen more. Rein in your magic and your mind."

Which only leaves me my muscle. Even that she'd have me hide away from the world.

"They call me a bastard," I blurt out. "Did you know that?"

Her eyes widen almost imperceptibly.

"They call me a bastard and you a whore. That's why my knuckles are always bloody. I'm fighting for your honor." My anger is beginning to get the better of me, which is problematic. And under my mother's roof, I had to live by two hard and fast rules: one, I must never use my magic, and two, I must control my temper. I'm decent at the former and shit at the latter.

She turns to our sad pot of beets. "You are not a bastard," she says, so softly I barely hear it over the bubbling cauldron.

But I do hear it.

My heart nearly stops.

Not…a bastard? Not a misbegotten? The entire axis of my universe shifts in an instant.

"I'm not a bastard?"

Slowly, her eyes move from the pot back to me. I swear I see a flash of regret. She hadn't meant to tell me.

"No," she finally says, her expression turning resolute.

My heartbeat begins to pick up speed at an alarming rate, and I have the oddest urge not to believe her. This is the kind of talk you sit your son down for; you don't just casually slip it into the conversation.

I stare at her, waiting for more.

She says nothing.

"Truly?" I press.

She takes a shaky breath. "Yes, Desmond."

Something that feels an awful lot like hope surges through me. Bastards live tragedies. Sons live sagas. All my mother's books are very clear on that point.

I am some man's son. His *son.* Masculine pride rushes through me, though it's quickly doused by reality. I am still the boy raised by a single mother, and I have lived a fatherless existence. Perhaps I'm no bastard, but the world still sees me as one, and knowing my mom's love of secrets, the world will continue to see me as one even after today.

"Did he die?"

How? How did our lives come to this?

She shakes her head, refusing to look at me.

"Then he abandoned us."

"No, my son."

What other answer is left?

The only one that comes to me has me scrutinizing my mother, my hardworking mother who keeps many, many secrets and who has taught me to do the same.

"You left him," I state. Of course. It's the only logical answer left.

She grimaces, still refusing to look at me, and there is my answer.

"You left him and took me with you."

It feels like someone's stacked stones in my stomach. This sense of loss is almost unbearable, mostly because I didn't know I had anything *to* lose in the first place.

"Who was my father?"

My mother shakes her head.

This is the kind of revelation that I shouldn't have to pull teeth to get.

"Tell me. You owe me that." I can feel my magic hammering beneath my skin, begging for release. A name is all I need.

Again, she shakes her head, her brows furrowed.

"If you have *any* love for me, then you'll tell me who he is." Then I could find him, and he could claim me as his son, and all those kids who called me a bastard would realize I had a father...

My magic builds and builds. I can feel it crawling up and down my back, pressing against the skin there.

"It's *because* I love you that I won't tell you," she says, her voice rising in agitation.

This is where I'm supposed to drop the subject. But this is my *father* we're talking about, one whole half of my identity that's been missing all my life. She's treating this conversation like it doesn't matter.

"What kind of answer is that?" I say hotly, my annoyance turning into anger. My power becomes frenzied at the taste of my heated emotions. Harder it presses against my back, becoming an itch.

"Desmond," she says sharply, "if you knew the truth, it could kill you."

My heart beats faster. Sharp, sharp pressure at my back.

Who is my father? I need to know!

"You're the one who's always droning on about educating

myself," I throw at her. "That 'knowledge is the sharpest blade,'" I say, quoting her. "And yet you still won't tell me my father's identity." My words lash out, and with them I feel the skin of my back give.

I groan as the flesh parts, and my magic shoves its way out of me. I have to bend over from the force of it, leaning my hand on the nearby counter.

My wings are sprouting, I think, distantly. My back throbs, tingling with my magic, and it's not quite pain but it isn't exactly pleasant either. My power consumes me, darkening my vision and making my body shake.

Didn't know it would be like this.

I sense rather than see my mother turning away from the cauldron to give me her full attention. This is about the time I get a verbal lashing. And then her form stiffens as she takes me in.

I breathe heavily between waves of magic.

Why, now of all times, did my wings have to sprout?

They tug at my back, and they should feel heavy, but my magic is making them buoyant, about the weight they'd be if I were submerged in water.

I blink, trying to bring the room into focus. My sight sharpens for a moment, and I see my mother clearly.

Her eyes are wide as they gaze at my wings. She takes a shaky step back, nearly knocking into the heated cauldron.

"You have his wings," she says, sounding utterly terrified.

Her form slips out of focus, and my attention unwillingly turns inward. I fight against it, determined to finish the conversation.

"*Whose* wings?" I say, my voice sounding very far away to my own ears. I feel like I'm in another room. My magic pulses *tha-thump, tha-thump, tha-thump* inside me.

I don't hear her answer, and I'm not entirely sure whether that's because she never spoke, or I simply didn't hear it over the *whoosh* of power deafening my ears.

"Tell me and I'll swear to the Undying Gods never to tell."

My power begins to ebb, the darkness clearing from my vision. I make out my mother, and she gives me the same sort of pitying look all the townspeople give me.

"My son, that is not a vow you can keep," she says softly, her voice breaking. Her terror and her pity are giving way to a more hopeless expression, something that looks a lot like desolation.

She's not going to tell me—not today and from her expression, probably not anytime soon. She'd have me endure the taunts and insults for years more. All so that she can shelter me. As though I'm a defenseless babe!

My anger rises swiftly within me, dragging my power along with it.

…You are a man now…

I am. My wings are proof enough of that. My wings and my magic, the latter of which is building on itself, darkening my vision once more. My wings flare out, so large I can't fully extend them in our cramped quarters.

Too much magic.

I sway on my feet. My anger amplifies my power, and my power, in turn, amplifies my anger, building to some elusive crescendo.

Can't control it.

I know a split second before I lose control that my magic is too big for my body and too strong for my will.

And then the storm trapped beneath my veins is trapped no more.

"*Tell me.*" My voice booms, my power rippling across the room. Our dining table slides across the floor, the chairs tumbling. The kitchen utensils hanging over our cauldron now fly across the room, and our crude stoneware plates shatter against the far wall.

It's a testament to my mother's strength that my power only manages to make her stumble back a few feet. My dark power coils around her. I can actually *see* it, like tendrils of inky smoke.

As soon as I release my magic out into the room, it loosens its hold on me. Again I can think clearly.

Horror replaces anger. Never have I spoken to my mother this way. Never has my power slipped its leash—though never has my power felt so *vast*.

I can still see my magic in front of me. It circles my mother's throat and seeps into her skin.

I feel sick as I watch her throat work.

What have I done?

…Don't you know…

…Can't you feel it…

…You've compelled her to answer…

Gods' bones. Now I can feel it, like a phantom limb. My magic is clawing its way through my mother's system, prying the secret from her.

Something flickers in her eyes, something alarming, something that looks an awful lot like fear.

Fear of *me*.

She fights the words, but eventually she loses.

"Your father is Galleghar Nyx."

CHAPTER 2
THE SHADOW KING

254 years ago

"They're coming." My mother slams our cavern door closed as she storms into our house.

"Who?" I close the book I've been reading and slide my ankles off the edge of the table. I'm not supposed to kick my feet up on our table, and normally I'd get chewed out for it, but today, my mom doesn't even notice.

"Your father's men."

I look at my mother with alarm as she grabs my arm, dragging me toward the back recesses of our home where our rooms are. Every room in our house has a door or an artificial wall to seal the caverns we dwell in from those that lie beyond. The entire heart of Arestys is a maze of them, spanning nearly the length of the island. Not even I know all of the caverns by heart, and I've lived my whole life inside them.

"Why are the king's men coming?" I ask, my voice deepening in alarm.

Control your emotions, I tell myself, though it's my mother's voice I hear in my head. For fairies, power and emotion are all wrapped up together. Lose control of one, and you'll lose control of the other.

And if the king's men are coming, I can't afford to lose control.

Since the day three years ago that my mom confessed my father was *the* Galleghar Nyx, tyrant King of Night, I sealed away all dreams of reuniting with him. Better to be a bastard than his son.

Galleghar Nyx is a powerful man. A cruel, powerful man. The kind of man you hope never notices you.

"Someone saw your wings," she says.

I swallow. My distinctive, *damning* wings. Fairies don't tend to have the talon-tipped wings of dragons and demons. In fact, there's only one particular line of fairies that share this trait—the royal bloodline.

I had the misfortune of inheriting my father's wings.

"They must've reported them," she continues.

Fear coils low in my stomach. I did this. Over the last three years, I've kept my wings hidden, but sometimes even my practiced control slips.

"I'm sorry," I say, running a hand through my white hair. The words sound hollow. It's easy enough to apologize for a mistake, but this is so much bigger than a simple mistake.

Too many fights that I went looking for and too many pretty women I spent too long gazing after. I baited myself over and over again with the exact things that triggered my wings.

And there had been that village girl the other week… she'd seen them. She'd seen them and all but ran to tell the village elders. I was only able to stop her by striking a bargain—her silence for a bracelet made out of moonbeams and asteroid hearts.

I can't wield magic, but I've gotten good at churning out deals.

So I whispered to the sweet moon stories about the sun until she shared a little of her light, and I let the cosmos taste my essence in return for the hearts, and it took four days, but I got the village girl her heavenly bracelet.

Apparently it was all for nothing. She must've told someone in those four days before I could fulfill my end of the bargain. After all, it's not every day that you stumble upon the heir to the Night Kingdom.

"Don't apologize for who you are," my mother says now, refusing to allow me to take the fall for something that is surely my fault. She drags me to her room, shutting the door behind her.

"Your powers are still awakening?" she asks, changing the subject.

I nod. I was powerful before my wings sprouted, and even though I gained a huge portion of my magic that night, it's been steadily burgeoning within me ever since.

The look my mother gives me is both proud and full of worry. "My son, you're already powerful. Not yet powerful enough to escape your father's clutches, but one day…one day you might become the very thing he fears."

I don't know what to do with her words. At any other time I might preen under the praise, but right now…they sit like spoiled meat in my stomach.

She releases my hand and moves over to her rickety bed. She pushes it aside, staring at the ground beneath it. I follow her gaze, looking at the uneven, rocky surface. Other than some dust motes, there's nothing to be seen.

She holds her hand out and mutters a few words under her breath. My arms prickle as I feel her magic drift out from her. The ground shimmers, like a mirage, then disappears, revealing a huge pit in its place. And inside the pit...

"Mom...?"

I stare, transfixed, at the mountain of coins that fill it nearly to the brim. Some are copper, some are silver, but most are gold. Scattered between them are rough cut gemstones, the kind that pulse with heartbeats.

Lapis viventem. Alchemist stones.

"What—what is all this?" I ask.

There's far more money here than a scribe makes. Whatever my mother has been doing, it's not just scribbling out the histories of Arestys.

My mother stares at the treasure. "It's yours," she says, her gaze moving to me.

Her words are like a blow to the chest. She's been saving all this money...for me?

I'm shaking my head. Fairies don't give gifts like this, not without catches. Not even to their brood.

It feels like cursed magic.

"I won't take it."

"You *will*, my son," she says, "along with the rest of your inheritance."

I furrow my brows as I look at her. There's more?

She looks steadily at me. "My secrets."

My heart is pounding, and whatever she's about to say, I don't want to hear it because *secrets are meant for one soul to keep.*

I pinch my eyes shut and shake my head over and over again. I refuse to think of what it means that she's breaking one of her deepest rules. That she's giving me her *inheritance.* That's an ominous word to use.

"Desmond," she says, touching my shoulder and shaking me slightly, "where is the man I raised? I need you to be strong for me right now."

My eyes open at her words, and I'm silently begging her to not go down this path, but she ignores my look.

"The King of Day owes me a favor. Take this money, buy yourself asylum."

Asylum? In the Kingdom of Day? Forced to never see the night?

"If he won't accept your money, tell him you're the daughter of Larissa Flynn and Galleghar Nyx. Show him your wings if you need to. He will not refuse you then."

"Only if you come with me," I say. Because that seems to be the catch—acquire safety, but abandon my mother. And that I will not do.

She cups my cheek. "I can't, my son. I bought my fate long ago."

I squint at her, not understanding.

"Listen carefully," she says, "because I only have time to tell you this once. I didn't love your father—I never did," she says.

As soon as the words leave her mouth, I still. So many times I imagined asking her about this—how she came into my father's clutches. I couldn't fathom how my clever, principled mother could care for the Shadow King, a man who collected wives and killed his children.

"My name once was Eurielle D'Asteria. Originally, I was one of the king's spies," she admits.

My mother? A spy? *Secrets are meant for one soul to keep* is an apt slogan for a spy...

"I didn't answer directly to him," she continues, "so for many decades we never came face-to-face. Not until I foiled an assassination attempt on the king did he ever lay eyes on me."

My mother saved the king's life. That revelation leaves a bitter taste in my mouth. There are urchins more worthy of saving than the creature that rules our land.

"Galleghar invited me to his palace to personally medal me for the deed." Her eyes grow distant. She shakes her head. "I should have known better than to go, but go I did. That day I entered that meeting a spy, but by the end of it, I'd been stripped of my title and duties, and I was deposited into his harem."

I raise my eyebrows. "Why?" I ask, bewildered. From everything I've read, fairies don't just choose mates over the course of a day. Some circle each other for centuries before settling down.

My mother lifts a shoulder. "He never really told me."

So he ripped her life from her and forced her to be his. The thought makes my skin crawl.

I'm a product of that union.

"I was with him for many years, many long, lonesome years. Until, one day, things changed.

"Galleghar doesn't let his concubines have much freedom, but on one rare occasion I was outside the palace walls, enjoying a traveling fair, when a diviner told me a piece of my future."

My mother pauses. "She said, 'In your hour of desperation, you'll know what to do, and the world will thank you for it.'

"I forgot the diviner's words until the day I found out I was pregnant. It was only then that they came back to me. And she was right, I did know what to do. I sold off centuries of my life for the means to escape, and eventually, I fled the king's palace right under his nose. I came here, and here I've stayed ever since."

My mother sold off centuries of her life?

She clasps the side of my face. "So you see, my son, my fate was decided long before today."

My heart is squeezing and squeezing. I imagine this is how a star feels as it dies, like everything it loves and everything it is, is pressing inwards and crushing the life out of it.

I shake my head in her hands. My eyes are starting to sting, but I'm still too shocked to fully process all that my mother has said.

She pulls my face in close. "Hide your wings, control your temper, and learn everything you can about the world, starting with your enemies," she breathes. "Trust no one, and above all, don't share your secrets."

———

My mother is still cradling my face when we hear the thud of footsteps echo down the caverns.

The two of us share a wild look.

My father's men are here.

"There's a bag amongst your inheritance that's spelled to hold it all. Collect what you can while I hold the soldiers off, and then leave." She nods to the door at the back of her room, the one that leads out to the maze of tunnels behind our house.

I shake my head. "Only if you come with me," I insist stubbornly.

"Desmond," she says calmly, "you are a king's son. A legitimate heir to a tyrant's kingdom. You need to keep yourself alive not just for my sake, or yours, but for our realm's. Do you understand?"

"*Stop*," I say hoarsely, because I do understand, but I don't want to.

She releases me, backing toward the door that leads out of her bedroom and into our living room. "I love you, my son. Till darkness dies, I will."

My heart thunders.

Up until now, this has been my life. These slick, dank cave walls, this humble abode, this enigmatic mother. I've resented this life for years, but now, right when I might lose it all, I find I can't bear the thought. Not my mother's sacrifice, not my cursed situation, not the possibility that this might all come to a swift end because this life, even as bleak as it is, is somehow too good for the likes of us.

I stare at the chest of coins. Years' worth of riches my mother worked for, all so that one day she could save me, and me alone.

She's almost to the door when I realize that I suddenly can't agree to this. To any of it.

Need to beat her to those soldiers.

I call on my magic, and it rises within me as though I'd been using it all along. For years I rejected it, but even after all that time it hasn't forsaken me.

I have no idea how to handle my power, but it doesn't seem to matter. All I have to do is will myself to stop my mother, and my magic responds.

One moment, I'm a man, and in the next, skin, bone, and muscle bleed away. All that's left of me is conscious thought. In an instant I'm one with the darkness.

I move across the room, and I don't even have time to feel wonder or fright that I can do this—that I can become the night—before I reappear between my mother and the door out, my body forming into that of a man once more.

Her eyes widen as she takes me in.

"I'm sorry," I say, my hand going to the doorknob. In the distance I can hear the clomp of soldiers' boots growing louder, "but you didn't raise a coward."

Before she has a chance to react, I open the door and slip out.

Bar the door.

Once again my power rises to accommodate me, and the door slams closed, sealing shut behind me.

I almost laugh at how easy it is to use my magic. So much easier than containing it like I've always had to do.

"Desmond!" My mom's muffled voice sounds panicked as she jiggles the doorknob. Her power batters against mine as she throws spells at the door, but even unpracticed as I am at magic, I can tell I'm stronger than her. Much stronger. That door isn't going to budge anytime soon.

Now it's my mother who will be forced to escape out the back of her room and me who will face down my father's men.

Good.

They're after me anyway.

———————

Behind me, the door to my mother's room rattles.

"*Desmond!*" she cries out again.

I ignore her, crossing our living room and heading for the front door. I can still hear the soldiers' footfalls, and by the sounds of it, they haven't yet reached our house.

I open our front door, and at the other end of the dark tunnel that leads to our house I see a squadron of soldiers heading down the dank passageway. It's then and only then that I realize I don't have a plan.

As soon as they see me, the uniformed men and women begin to run down the tunnel, toward our home, their hands dropping to their swords. This will be no civil visit. In that instant I truly understand that having the king's blood running through me is a death sentence.

But it also makes me strong. Very strong.

I square my shoulders and widen my stance. My mother is not sacrificing herself today. Not on my behalf.

Stop them.

My magic snaps out of me, rippling across the cave and bending the light before it slams into the soldiers.

They're blasted off their feet and then thrown onto their backs, every last one toppling over like felled trees. No one gets up.

The silence that follows is deafening.

Did I...kill them?

But as I watch, one of them moves his arm and another sighs out a breath.

My muscles relax. Unconscious, but not dead.

I back away, moving into my house, using my power rather than my hand to close my front door.

Time to go.

I make my way back across the living room toward my mother's bedroom. It's only as I lay my hand on the doorknob that I realize it's quiet. Far too quiet.

Unease slices through me as I open that door.

Beyond it, my mother's room is exactly how I left it, save for three things: my inheritance is hidden again, the back door is open, and my mother is gone.

She fled, I tell myself. But the hairs on the back of my neck are standing on end, and there's a taste to the air...

Hostile magic.

This time, I become one with the darkness before I can even think the command, disappearing from my mother's room and reappearing right outside her back door.

A short way away I can hear voices, and my mother's is one of them.

Cold, clammy fear takes root low in my stomach, and it's spreading like a vine through me.

Cautiously, I become one with the darkness again, vanishing in one instant, and materializing behind a slimy, mineralized column a moment later.

From where I stand, I can see my mother, her back to me, and across from her…

My blood runs cold.

I see my hair, my eyes, and my jawline all worn by another man, a man I've read about so many times I feel like I know him. He's a man I've come to loathe.

My father, Galleghar Nyx, the King of Night.

———

I stare at the tyrant king of our realm.

Galleghar's white hair halos his face; it looks like he's run his fingers through it far too many times. His black outfit is heavily adorned with gold, his boots so highly polished they shine like mirrors.

His face is inarguably handsome in a cruel sort of way, and from his imposing stature it's obvious that he's not just magically gifted but also physically dominant.

…*monstrous man*…

…*murders babes*…

…*tortures innocents*…

…*hunts mortals*…

…*makes even the darkness weep*…

The shadows gossip; even they have no loyalty to their king.

All around Galleghar fairy lights hang in the air, though I get the impression he doesn't need light to see in the dark.

"Eurielle D'Asteria," he says, "my fallen star."

Whether it's those words or that voice, my blood runs cold.

"For seventeen years you evaded me." His eyes drink her in.

A protective instinct in me flares to life when I see the way he stares at her. Like he wants to possess her.

"I looked everywhere. Questioned everyone. Followed every lead. But they were all dead ends." He begins to pace, never taking his eyes off my mother. "My favorite wife vanished from my palace, hours after I attended her, and it was as though she never existed in the first place." He snaps his fingers and opens his palms as if to demonstrate the act of disappearing.

My mother doesn't respond, just watches the king.

"In fact, when I tried to track down your family, your friends—anyone who came before me—I found they never existed at all. There were fake names for imaginary people. Imagine my surprise when I discovered a spy employed into the royal house had a resume built on lies. A spy that became my wife."

"*You* chose *me*, Galleghar," she says quietly, finally breaking the silence.

He laughs, and worlds should tremble at that terrible sound. "I did, didn't I?" His smile disappears. "I do like clever creatures—and how clever you were. It took you one night to deceive me." He holds his index finger up. "Just one."

He takes a couple steps closer to her, his footsteps

echoing throughout the cavern. I can tell just by the way the air darkens at his back—right where his wings should be—that he's angry and exhilarated all at once.

"I should've known," he continues. "You did warn me how much you loved keeping secrets." He narrows his eyes. "There's one secret in particular I'm curious about. You see, when a report came to me a few days ago concerning your whereabouts," he steps in close to her, his voice dropping to a menacing pitch, "it said I have a son."

My body stills, fear roaring through my veins. My magic pushes against the underside of my skin, begging to be set loose.

I need to act, I need to save my mother, but the King of the Night is rumored to be one of the most powerful fairies in existence. There's no way I can subdue him. But every moment I hesitate is another moment wasted. How can I possibly get my mother and me out of here?

"Well?" he pushes. "Is it true?"

Even from what little I can see of my mother, I can tell she's lifted her chin. "What use is my word, Galleghar? Haven't we already established that I'm a liar?"

The Night King eyes her shrewdly. He's about to do something, I can sense it. There's so much pent-up aggression behind his eyes, and he wants to unleash it. *Needs* to unleash it.

I'm about to reveal myself when he drags his gaze away from my mother and looks at the caves that surround us. I duck back behind the column just before his gaze moves over the section of the cavern I'm in. Whatever his malevolent intentions are, he reins them in.

"So, this whole time, this is where you've been? Arestys' caves? No wonder I never found you. Even the lowliest slave wouldn't willingly subject themselves to this shithole."

"How it must wound you then," my mother says, her voice lilting, "to know I chose this over you."

His eyes snap back to her. He stares at her for a second, and then he flicks his wrist. A burst of his magic blasts into her, and my mother is viciously thrown to the cavern floor.

I swear my heart stops for a moment, and then my fury rises, drowning my fear. It rushes through my veins, thicker than blood.

No one lays a hand on my mother.

I step out from behind the column, my magic making the shadows gather around me.

"I came here planning to kill you," the king continues. His entire focus is so fixed on my mother that he doesn't see me, even though I'm in plain sight. He has eyes only for her.

Kneeling down, he threads a hand through her hair and jerks her head up to face him. "But on second thought, perhaps I'll keep you and let you live. Perhaps every night I'll let you choose the man who will force himself on you."

My power is building on itself, my wrath fueling it. I take a step forward, and then another, but neither of them notices. They only have hate-filled eyes for each other.

My mother laughs in the king's face, mocking his threat. "So long as it's not you attending me, I welcome the punishment."

The hairs on my arm rise. Both my mother's words and her voice sound different. I've always thought she was soft, but she's not. Gods, is it clear to me now more than ever that she's not. She's whoever she wants to be—loving mother, royal spy, reluctant concubine, clumsy scribe. And beneath all her masks is a woman that should make men quake.

The king reels back, rising to his feet, just as shocked by her words as I am.

I see the moment that shock melts away, the cruel lines of his face sharpening. His anger is so like mine. It churns right beneath the surface, gathering force.

No wonder my mother stared at me so fearfully all those years ago when I lost control of my own anger and my power lashed out of me. No wonder she's drilled into me the need for control. She saw what I'm only now seeing—

I am my father's son.

"Anyone but me?" he says. "Is that it? You're used to servicing slaves and thieves?" That anger of his is mounting. "Perhaps if I am so bad, then I should do the honors." His hand reaches for his belt, and that's all I can take.

Before I know what I'm doing, I'm propelling through the darkness. I materialize in front of my father, my body still hurtling forward, my fist cocked back. An instant later I slam it into his face, roaring as I do so. I throw all my rage, all my fear, and a healthy dose of my power into the hit.

He goes flying through the air, his body colliding with a pillar that shatters against his back.

I mean to grab my mother and run, but this is my father. The father who degraded her, threatened her, *struck* her. The same father I once pined for. The man my mother has protected me from. The man whose cursed blood runs through my veins.

I feel that potent, rotten blood of ours. It's enticing me to be vicious, to end what I started. And I still have too little control of my own anger to resist my magic.

I straighten my shoulders, my wings fanning open behind me.

"*Desmond*," my mother says behind me, "*don't*."

Ignoring her, I stride over to my father, the darkness gathering around me as I watch him sit up. I step up to him just as he wipes away a line of blood seeping from the corner of his mouth.

He stares up at me, his eyes moving to my wings. "So the rumors were true." Then his gaze moves over my frame, which I know is slender and wiry, then my face. "Pity you are not much to look at."

I say nothing, though my jaw clenches.

The two of us lock eyes, our rage moving like a river beneath our skin.

Finally, my father flashes a cruel smile. "Yes, you are my son indeed. That power is a terrible burden, isn't it?"

I'm not sure I could answer him if I wanted to. I need to release this magic before it devours me.

My mother's hand clasps my shoulder, breaking the spell. "Leave him, Desmond," she says quietly.

But not quietly enough.

The king's eyes move to my mother. "Leave me?" he says, his eyes narrowing, even as he begins to grin. "You think I'd let either of you escape me twice?"

One second my father is in front of me, the next he's gone.

I startle.

Same power as mine.

That's all I have time to think before my mother's hand is ripped from my shoulder.

I swivel around in time to see the king at her back, a knife to her throat.

He doesn't hesitate. Faster than I can react, he drags the blade across her delicate neck, slicing the throat of the only person I've ever cared about.

Time seems to stop. *Everything* seems to stop.

My entire life condenses to this one instant, this one terrible instant. And it can't be real. None of this can be real.

Not that blood, which spills down her throat like some strange necklace. Not my mother's surprised face, or her choked breath, which bubbles out of her wound. Not my father's pleased face and his wrathful eyes.

This…this can't be possible.

All at once, time whooshes back to life, and I realize this is possible. This is real. This is what death looks like. This is what true, endless loss feels like.

I'm still that dying star, all my magic, all my grief, all my fury and fear pressing inward. The pressure of it all builds until it's unbearable. The cavern darkens with it.

I stare at my mother, and I can barely feel the hot tears tracking down my face.

My eyes move to my father.

Everything silences—my pain, my power, my dying heart. I can only hear my breath sighing in and out of me.

And then my magic detonates.

My power explodes around me, the shock wave rippling out. My father only has a second to see me with horror-filled eyes before he winks out of existence, leaving the caverns in an instant.

My magic vaporizes everything in its path. The rock, the rubble, the home I was raised in, the fortune my mother saved for me, the soldiers still lying unconscious outside our front door, the tunnels I called home for the last sixteen years—it all disintegrates the moment my magic touches it, gone as though it never were.

My hair and clothes whip about me, caught up in the vortex of my power. And still it pours out of me. I can't hear anything over the deafening roar of it. It's in my ears, in my head, in my heart. It builds faster than my anger, swells larger than my anguish, and cuts deeper than my pride. It's a sea, and I'm drowning in it, getting sucked farther and farther down into that abyss, that dark, dark abyss.

Just as I feel it's about to consume me, the magic dies away.

For several seconds all I can do is take shallow breaths, the sound of air whistling in and out of my lungs deafening in the eerie silence that follows.

I sway on my feet, blinking as I take in the sight around me.

Gone. Everything is…gone. The caves, the soldiers, the king.

I stare up at the night sky above me, a sight I yearned for all those years I lived in a windowless house.

And then my eyes land on my mother. She's the only thing left untouched by my power.

But even she is gone.

I stumble over to her, falling to my knees at her side. I gather her to me, cradling her body in my arms. Her beautiful, violet eyes stare sightlessly past me, her neck gaping open.

"No, Mom…" My voice breaks.

In a matter of seconds, her blood coats my arms and stains my clothes.

There—there must be a way to undo this.

My eyes fall to her neck wound. I press a shaky hand to it, willing my magic to heal her. Nothing happens. I try again and get the same result. Maybe I used up all of my power earlier, maybe I'm no healer.

Or maybe it's just too late.

Some strange, wordless sound bubbles up my throat. Because it *is* too late.

No pulse, no breath, no life.

She's gone. *She's gone.*

Above me, the stars twinkle down.

She's gone and the stars still twinkle.

I let out an agonized cry, and then another, and another. And then my cries become sobs. I bow my head over her broken body, holding her close. If I could, I'd claw my heart out. It hurts so godsdamned bad.

I bury my face in my mother's neck. I feel her already cooling blood smear across my cheek and into my hair.

I don't know how long I hold her to me. Hours or minutes might have passed. My grief can't distinguish the difference. At some point my sobs taper off, replaced by a heavy, aching numbness.

And then, my skin prickles.

My shoulders tense when I sense hot gazes on my back. I know without looking that the townspeople have come to investigate. My wings are still out. My mother is still cradled in my arms. Still dead.

It doesn't matter anymore. None of it matters anymore. I have no mother, no house, no fortune, no future.

People begin to whisper behind me, and I can practically feel their curiosity and their fear. My entire life, they thought me a bastard, a poor, magicless bastard. Only now are they seeing my true lineage and power.

Just a day ago this would've felt vindicating. Now their eyes feel intrusive.

One of them messaged the king. Told him of my existence. One of them *caused* this. Whether it was that village girl, or her father, or someone else who saw something they shouldn't have. They told the king I lived. Surely they knew he'd come for me, surely they knew their words would doom us.

I stand slowly, my mother still in my arms, then turn to face them.

"Who did this?" I say slowly, my eyes moving over the faces of the gathering crowd. "Who wrote to the king about me and my mother?"

No one speaks, though many of them begin to shift uneasily, their eyes moving between me and one another.

"*Who did this?*" I shout again, my power sweeping out of me. Fairies scream as it knocks them to the ground.

My distinctive wings flare out. For once in my life, I deliberately keep them exposed. Those who haven't seen them yet now get a good long look at them. I see their eyes widen fearfully.

No one comes forward. I stare at each one of their faces, and this is the moment when they all realize that the boy they thought I was, was a mirage. That this entire time they've been the field mice and I've been the viper lying in the grass.

"I swear on my mother's grave," I say, my voice ringing out in the night, "I will find which one of you did this, and I will *make—you—pay.*" The earth shakes with my words, and again, people gasp, their faces terrified.

I glance up at the stars. There is one other fairy who needs to pay. One other who deserves the bulk of my wrath.

Without further thought, I bend my knees and spring into the sky, my mother still clasped to me. My wings beat at my back, and for the first time in my life, I force them to fly.

I grit my teeth as they propel me into the air, and at first sheer willpower and a bit of magic keeps me airborne. But then instinct takes over, and my wings begin to move as though I'd done this a hundred times.

I'm heading for the stars above me, and I don't look back at my small town with its small people full of small dreams.

Wrongs must be righted. A king must pay.

And realms will fall for my vengeance.

CHAPTER 3
THE ANGELS OF SMALL DEATH

254 years ago

It takes a day for me to bury my mother and another to leave her.

She rests among the ruins of Lyra, one of the oldest temples dedicated to the goddess of new life, her body nestled amongst Lyra's undying flowers. The story of the ancient goddess was always one of her favorites.

I stare at the freshly turned earth, my jaw locked hard.

She shouldn't be buried here, in an unmarked grave in the land of Flora. But I can't go back to Arestys, and that's the only home I've ever shared with my mother. So I leave her to her final sleep in a land I've only ever read about.

As I fly away from her grave and the distance between us grows larger and larger, my anger and pain smolder deep within me.

I feel my identity tearing apart, refashioning itself into something harder, colder. There's no more room in my heart for softness. I have one reason for existing, and one alone: to kill the king.

My mother wanted me to seek asylum in the Day Kingdom, but that was before, when my mother had saved up riches to give the King of Day. What are the chances that he'd take me in now, when I'm penniless?

I already know the answer.

She wouldn't have saved up the money if I didn't need it.

Which means that the last sixteen years of her savings, of us living off beet stew and sleeping in Arestys's caves, was all for nothing.

All. For. Nothing.

The unfairness of it burns through me, along with guilt. Thick, oily guilt that I could destroy everything my mother worked so hard for in an instant.

I'm a wanted man, and there's no place for me to go—

My wings almost freeze midbeat as a realization slams into me.

Of course.

There *is* a place that might welcome a bloodstained, penniless fairy. A place where violence and vendettas are born.

The City of Thieves. Barbos.

———

I sit inside some disreputable pub in Barbos, nursing the dregs of the last ale I can afford. I don't have enough money in my pocket for much more than another meal. I'll have to sleep on a rooftop tonight and hope no one discovers me before morning.

I glance around at the colorful fairy lights that are strung up along the walls of the place, then to the crowded room.

Friends gather around tables, their eyes a little too all-seeing, and their smiles a bit too crafty.

Sitting amongst thieves.

How I'd once dreamed of coming to such a place. All I ever wanted growing up was to see the world and live the lives that I'd read about for so long. Now it feels like I bought myself one of Memnos's cursed wishes—the kind that give you anything you want, but corrupt the wish so that it becomes a burden rather than a boon.

I nearly choke on my next swallow of ale when a fae woman in a translucent top wanders into the pub. She sashays rather than walks, her eyes brighter than the stars outside. I can't look away from her, though I know I should.

She weaves her way between tables, her fingers skimming along the sticky surfaces. The woman must feel my gaze because her eyes flick to me. She flashes me a smile, and the sight of it is so shocking that I stare a little longer. Back on Arestys, despite my looks and my penchant for getting people what they wanted, I was no woman's first choice of partner. No one wanted to openly show interest in the weakest fairy on the island. I was always the mistake village girls liked to make when they were feeling brave.

Before the woman gets to my table, a slick-looking fairy carrying two steins of ale drops into the seat across from me, jolting me out of my reverie.

He leans forward. "Trust me, you don't want that kind of company," he says, jerking his head back to the woman. Over his shoulder he says to her, "Fuck off, Kaelie. This bloke won't be buying what you have to offer."

Buying…?

The woman's smile turns to a scowl. "Damnit, Vale, you owe me for that."

The pub's other patrons ignore us. I guess this isn't a noteworthy altercation in Barbos.

Vale turns in his seat to look at her. "Piss off," he says. "He's got no money and he's younger than your sons—or are you too blind to see that?"

Giving Vale a look that could kill the Night King himself, she slips away from us, circling through the tavern until a brawny fairy grabs her by the waist and pull her onto his lap.

Vale turns back to face me, taking a sip of his drink and making himself comfortable.

I raise my eyebrows at him.

He takes in my expression. "Have you never seen a prostitute?"

No, but that's beside the point.

"Why are you sitting here?" I ask.

He slides his second ale over to me. "You look lonely, brother."

I frown. I'm not his brother. My siblings lie in shallow graves across the Night Kingdom, and I buried the last of my family a day ago.

I eye the stein he passed to me.

"Go ahead, you can have it," he says, cajoling me.

"What do you want?" I ask.

Vale leans back in his seat, the wooden chair creaking. "Company."

I cup the mug of ale I purchased. "If company's what you want, then you should've taken Kaelie up on her offer."

He lets out a rough laugh. "Aye, if I took Kaelie up on her offer, I'd be scratching my balls for weeks and praying to ye old gods for deliverance." He pushes the mug toward me a little more. "Drink up."

My eyes flick to it, then him. I'm not a babe; I know

enough about bargaining to know the moment I take a sip, I'll be in this man's debt.

I push the stein back toward him.

Leaning forward, he pushes it back. "I have a proposition," he says.

"Now you're propositioning me?" I ask, my brows nudging up again.

"Quick tongue on you," Vale says. "That's good—very good. Listen, I've seen your type, and I know wherever home is, you can't go back to it."

I tense a little, my mind replaying the last moments of my mother's life. My gaze sharpens on Vale; I'm unnerved by how well he can read me.

"I know you need money," he adds. "I want to help you."

I slide my stein from one hand to the other, passing it back and forth across the gummy table. "No one wants to help me," I say. "If you knew me better, you'd understand that."

Vale looks around and clears his throat. "All right, smart-arse, I'll give it to you straight," he says, lowering his voice. "I can get you a job—highly illegal—which involves moving goods. You'll get paid well," he says.

Finally, some truth.

"Are you interested?" he asks.

My hands still, my mug sliding to a halt. I stare down into my now empty drink, trying to divine my options. But I'm out of them. And if it breaks the Shadow King's laws, I'm all for it.

I look up at Vale. "Maybe."

Two hours later Vale leads me to a mansion down the street

from the pub. The house is situated along the rim of the island, the back of it facing toward the empty night sky.

"We're known around these parts as the Angels of Small Death—or the Brotherhood," he explains to me. "We're a band of men who can get the good people of the Night Kingdom certain *amenities* they might not otherwise be able to come by. And this is our headquarters." He gestures to the house ahead of us.

I stare up at the Goliath home, its vine-covered walls towering above me, the balmy night air stirring the shallow pools of water and the fronded palms that lead up to it.

Vale has me lingering outside the mansion for longer than necessary, letting me absorb the impressive wealth around me. I glance at him, my face impassive. All those years of control my mother drilled into me are now coming in handy. Because I am impressed—impressed and out of my depth. I'm just a poor boy from Arestys, whose only exposure to the Otherworld was through my mother's books. And up until a few days ago, I was a nobody.

Vale leads me into the house. Inside, the rooms are ostentatious. Every surface is covered in snowy, opalescent stone and carved into intricate designs. Near the ceiling, mini pinpricks of light twinkle from the darkness. Miniature clouds roll between them, passing by a small moon that's nearly full. It's obvious that the top of the room has been spelled to look like a dreamscape. This enchantment alone had to have cost a fortune.

As we snake our way through the house, we pass by several women clad in gold clothes and chains who silently recline on couches.

I come to a stop when I notice their ears.

Vale takes a few more steps before he realizes I'm not following.

I'm still staring at the women. Their eyes languidly move to me, but they don't budge.

"They're..."

"Human," Vale finishes for me, coming to my side. I can feel his greedy eyes on me, sensing an opening. "Have you ever tried human flesh?" he asks.

Of course I haven't. I've never even *seen* a human; I've only heard about them. In Arestys, everyone's too poor to own slaves. But not in Barbos.

I was told that humans were coarse, ugly things, but these women don't look all that different from fae women. They wear thick gold bands around their necks, their wrists, and ankles, the cuffs all linked together by thick, woven gold chains. I'd assumed the chains were fashionable adornments, but now I realize they're actually shackles.

The women look how I've felt my entire life. But it's more than what they wear. Their sad eyes pull at that grieving part of me. I understand their expressions, like they've lost something precious.

Vale pats me on the back. "Come."

My gut is twisting. I don't want to leave these women, even though I know I can't save them. I couldn't save my mother, and I sure as shit can't save myself.

Reluctantly I follow Vale out of the room.

A minute later we enter a large room made mostly out of a dark stone shot through with veins of gold. Sparking light glows dimly from the sconces along the walls. Stretching out in front of us are several pools full of glowing water. The light from it dances along the walls.

The air is heavy with steam and magic; it hangs in misty ribbons throughout the room and nestles itself in my lungs.

"It's imported from Lephys," Vale says.

"What is?"

"The water." He nods to the luminous liquid.

I follow his gaze. Several naked couples are tangled together suggestively in the waters, many with their wings out.

I look away before I can help it.

"Never seen fairies rut?" Vale asks, his eyes taking in every twitch of mine.

I force my face into some bland expression. On Arestys, I was cunning. Here I'm an ignorant dustback, an Arestyan with no exposure to the outside world. I hate that. I spent years educating myself on the Otherworld, all to avoid situations like this. It was all wasted effort.

Vale's lips stretch into a grin. "We can always change that, my brother. You'll find that in this line of business, you'll never be short of partners—willing or otherwise."

Or otherwise? My skin crawls. That's not a partner, that's a hostage.

Vale's grin disappears, and he leads me down the marble pathway that bisects two of the pools.

At the far end of the room is the largest pool yet, and it's filled with a single man and dozens of women.

The man's long black hair is plaited and fitted with jeweled ornaments.

…Pirate…

He leans back along the rim of the pool while the women flock around him.

My gaze moves from one woman to the next. Some have bare necks and pointed ears while others have rounded ears, their throats collared. More slaves.

44

Lazily, the man's eyes slide from the women to us.

"What's this?" he asks, studying me.

"Hermio," Vale says, dipping his head. "I found you our newest recruit."

I narrow my gaze on Vale, annoyed. "I've agreed to nothing," I say, my attention moving from him to Hermio, the man in the pool.

The man in the pool raises an eyebrow. "Where did you find him?" he asks Vale.

"Dead Dragon's Tavern. Boy was on his last few coppers."

My attention slides to Vale. Just how long had he been watching me?

"Mmmm…" Hermio purses his lips, looking me over, "he'll do. Get him outfitted and properly broken. I want him on the next job."

Properly broken? They're speaking as though I'm not even present!

…*Many bad things happen here…*

Vale's hand wraps around my upper arm, and he tries to pull me away. The touch is proprietary, like I'm already his subordinate.

I won't be someone else's agenda, and I'm not fucking falling into line.

I shrug off the fairy's hold. "I'm not interested," I say.

A human woman glides over to Hermio and begins stroking his hair. He leans his head back and closes his eyes. "Did Vale not explain the terms of your coming here?" he says.

I glance at Vale, whose face is expressionless, but I say nothing.

The mortal woman looks at me from the glowing waters, her eyes hollow. There's nothing behind them—not

45

fear, not love, not hate. She's an empty vessel, devoid of dreams and wants.

The sight is so disturbing that I siphon off a little of my magic, feed it to the darkness, and cast my questions to the shadows.

...stolen from earth...

...sold as slaves...

...His fortune was built on the lives of changelings...

Their answers sicken me.

Of course I knew that mortals were trafficked here, but that knowledge had been so far removed from my existence. Now, so soon after my mother's death, seeing these enslaved, *magicless* women reminds me of the childhood I endured.

My magic surges through me, called up by my outrage. My life up until now has been ruined by men like Hermio who use their power to crush those beneath them.

Why must the strong always hurt the weak?

Vale's eyes are on me, taking in my every reaction. I have to tamp my emotions down.

"Those who are invited here," Hermio says, "either leave our doors as brothers, or they don't leave at all."

The magic in the room rises, and suddenly, I sense dozens of fae eyes on me from across the room, and I feel the lick of hostile magic at my back. I'm being threatened in a chamber full of lawless fairies.

My anger and pain roil inside of me.

Never going to be weak again.

Giving Hermio and his women one last cursory glance, I turn on my heel and head back down the aisle, toward the exit. On either side of me, fairies watch idly.

The doors ahead of me slam shut, their thick wooden bars coming down heavily to further blockade them.

I stop in my tracks.

I look back over my shoulder at Hermio. "Unbar the doors."

The corner of his mouth lifts. "A penniless boy from... let me guess..."—his eyes flick over me—"*Arestys*, judging by the desperate look of your clothing, thinks he can stand up to me?"

Many of the other fairies in the room are slipping out of the pool, their wings flaring agitatedly.

Anger and anxiety build beneath my skin. My power begins to leak from me, and the already dim room begins to darken.

...*Yessss*...

Hermio tilts his head. "Now what is this? The poor beggar boy has a bit of magic to him." He clucks his tongue. "What a waste killing you will be."

My magic reaches one of the sparking fairy lights above us. It pulses once, then dims into darkness as the shadows swallow it up.

...*More*...

Another fairy light flickers before snuffing out.

Hermio waves his hand, and his men take that as a cue. They move toward me, their magic rippling across their skin.

"Don't kill him right away," Hermio says, the corner of his mouth lifting up as he takes me in. "Because he is young and foolish, I'm willing to let him reconsider my offer—after he learns his lesson, of course."

My hands begin to tremble as the fairies close in on me. A few of them notice, and they flash me menacing smiles.

They think I'm afraid of them. Fools. I'm afraid of my own capabilities. My mother taught me how to control my magic, not how to wield it. For all I know, it could either fail me or take out a block of Barbos. It's a coin toss which it will be.

The first of Hermio's men reach me, grabbing my arm.

Too late for worries now.

I close my eyes, lean my head back, and release my magic.

It's the easiest thing in the world. No, it's more than that. It's letting go when I've been holding on. I almost sigh as my magic charges out of me.

Sweet relief.

The fairy who grasps my arm is the first to be hit by it. He doesn't have time to scream when my shadowy power rushes over him. It rips him away from me and knocks him to the ground before engulfing him. My magic continues on, moving out like a wave and descending upon the fairies around me. Few have time to scream before my shadows devour them. A distant part of me can feel their bones breaking, their bodies disintegrating, their magic fueling the darkness ever onwards.

A few fairies are brave enough to throw their magic at me, and I can tell by the force of it that they are giving me all that they got. It dissolves uselessly against the wall of my own magic.

The men and women who still linger in the water—presumably those people who are here as entertainment rather than muscle—now flee from the pool, moving to the back of the room where Hermio is, their naked bodies glistening with glowing water droplets.

Not the slaves, I beseech my magic.

Astoundingly, it does as I ask, parting itself around the mortals as it lays siege to everything else.

The darkness extinguishes the fairy lights and eats up the illumination coming from the pools. Vale only has an instant to look terrified, and then there *is* no more Vale, just fairy dust and magical residue.

Finally, the shadows close in on Hermio. The leader of the Brotherhood isn't looking quite so regal as he scrambles out of the pool, turning around only to blast his power at me.

I'm actually impressed when the hit stops my shadows for a second. It's not enough to overpower my magic, but it is enough to encourage the kingpin. Hermio throws wave after wave of it at me, each hit weaker than the last.

I stride toward him, cloaked in my shadows.

He crouches at the back of the room, naked as the day he was born. "Please—no," he begs.

The darkness wants him; it's practically salivating for that powerful flesh. There's magic beneath that skin of his and it wants to touch it, taste it, *feed* from it.

My shadows converge on Hermio from all sides, swallowing him up. He begins to scream—a high-pitched, almost feminine sound—and then it cuts off prematurely.

The darkness is ravenous, tearing the fairy apart in seconds. It's not enough, not nearly enough, to satiate its appetite.

The shadows probe the exits, not ready to stop. They ooze through every crack and crevice they can find.

It's too much, the power pouring off me. My hold is slipping on my own dark magic, and I can't release it the way I did back in Arestys; it's not letting me.

...More, more, more...

...Let us live...

"No," I whisper, beginning to sweat as I fight to reel my power back in. The darkness blows the barred doors off their hinges. In the distance I hear surprised screams.

"No," I say again, my body trembling with exertion. "Stop."

The shadows blast away another hidden door at the back of the room.

A rivulet of sweat drips down my cheek. "Stop."

The darkness bounds into the surrounding rooms, and the shouts are beginning to build. If I don't end this now, I won't be a fairy that wields magic; I'll be magic that wields a fairy.

Control yourself, Desmond!

"*Stop!*" I roar.

The billowing darkness freezes. Then, all at once, it rushes back into my body, slamming against me like a leviathan.

I fall to my knees, choking on the magic.

By the time I catch my breath, the darkness clears. All that's left of the bathhouse's inhabitants are sparkling piles of ash where fairies once stood and a dozen mortals. Slowly, the slaves lift their heads, taking me in, their bodies shaking.

Several fae from nearby rooms rush in. When they see me, they stop in their tracks, their eyes taking everything in. If they want to kill me, I'm not sure at this point that I could stop them. But they don't try to kill me. Instead, one by one, they bend their knees and bow their heads.

I stare at them with no little amount of wonder and fear.

…They respect power…

And suddenly, the powerless boy from Arestys is powerless no more.

CHAPTER 4
A MORTAL MATE

252 years ago

I stare at my first tattoo beneath the bright, colorful lights of one of Barbos's seedier pubs. The angel gazes down my arm, her expression caught somewhere between mournful and serene.

Right at this moment my mood echoes hers. I rub my eyes.

"So you're officially a brother now?" Gladia, the barmaid who works here, slides a beer over to me, peering at the ink.

I've officially been one for two years now, but getting a tattoo is akin to marrying into the organization. My skin is now a testament to my loyalties, for better or for worse.

And I'm not sure how I feel about that.

Farther than ever from my revenge...

"Where *are* your brothers?" the barmaid asks.

Shaking down one of the king's officials.

I lean forward. "I could tell you"— eyes drop to Gladia's lips—"but then it would cost you."

Her eyes heat. "I'm willing to pay…"

An hour later I'm pulling on my pants. Below us I can hear the muffled sounds from the bar.

Gladia props her head up on the pillows. "Leaving so soon, Eurion?"

It's been two years since I'd adopted a fake name—all the better to evade my father with—but I still sometimes forget that I'm Eurion Nova and not Desmond Flynn.

Gladia reaches for me, and it's all I can do not to shake her touch off.

"I need to go."

Need might not be the right word, but the women I bed don't often want to hear the right words. Like the fact that Gladia is nothing more than a warm body. Or that I won't think of her again until the next time I see her.

I might no longer be a bastard by name, but I'm a bastard by deed.

"You smell like ale and sex," Malaki says when I enter the mansion later that evening.

He sees my sleeve, and whistles. "You got a tattoo." It's not exactly an accusation, but it might as well be. We'd planned on getting inked together.

In the end, like everything else in my life, I had to do it alone.

Phaedron storms through the room, his eyes locking on mine. "Where in all the realms have you been?" he says when he sees me. "I needed you an hour ago." His nose wrinkles. "You smell like woman," he growls. "Is that what you've been doing while your brothers waited for you? Wetting your prick?"

"I needed some time to think."

"Balls deep in some female?" Phaedron growls. "If you've

taken another lord's wife, I swear to the gods I won't bail you out this time. I'll let them take your head."

I'm not entirely sure I'd mind.

When his words elicit no reaction out of me, he sighs. "You and Malaki, get your arses to Memnos. We need to move our cursed water shipments within the next ten hours or the deal's off."

Fifteen minutes later, after I've rinsed myself off, Malaki and I leave the mansion together.

"You didn't need to wait for me," I tell him gruffly.

"What am I supposed to do, let you get into trouble all by yourself?"

I crack a smile.

The two of us are quiet for a minute. Then—

"Why do you put up with Phaedron's shit?" Malaki asks.

"He's the boss," I say simply.

"Only because you wouldn't take Hermio's place that night," Malaki says carefully.

That night.

The shadows, the screams, the fairy dust that remained behind.

I bid the memory away and look at my friend, really look at him. It took Malaki two years, but he finally decided to broach this subject.

"You think I should've," I state.

My friend gives me an incredulous look. "Of course I think you should've. Don't take offense, Eurion, but why else are you here? You killed off the Brotherhood's previous leader. Fairies only do that if they want to take over an establishment—or end it. But you did neither. Instead, you gave the position to Phaedron and became just another errand boy. Why?"

Because I had been beneath other fairies all my life, and

suddenly I was expected to be above them when I simply wanted to be *one of them*.

"Why not?" I respond.

Malaki shakes his head. "If I'd been given the chance to be a leader, I'd have taken it."

"I got what I wanted," I say.

"By stopping the skin trade into Barbos? You could've also done that as a leader—and you do realize that all you've done is given business to our rivals," he responds. "Remember that I can see into their heads when they sleep."

I stare grimly ahead of us. "Have you looked into mine?"

If he had, he'd learn just about every damnable secret of mine. My dreams love to parade my secrets around my mind.

Malaki reels back. "You know I haven't." He looks wounded by my question.

I shake my head. "If you had, you'd understand." If I was to survive in my father's kingdom, I had to stay anonymous. That meant no leadership roles, no grand gestures of power, no valiant deeds. All I needed was to stick to the shadows and scheme out my revenge.

"What's the issue with you today?" Malaki asks, searching my face.

I glance at him. Everyone who knows me understands I don't freely share much about myself.

I draw my eyes away from him to squint off in the distance. "Today's the anniversary of my mother's death."

A beat passes, then Malaki says, "Shit. I'm sorry. I didn't know."

I look up. "Nothing to apologize about."

And with that, I take to the sky, my wings enchanted to look like those of a drab gray moth.

It's only much later, after we've moved several crates of

Memnos's cursed waters to earth and returned to the Land of Nightmares, that Malaki and I have another chance to talk alone.

We wind through the streets of Memnos, the wilds of the island pressing in on all sides. Dark liquid slithers across the cobblestone road. I can feel the gazes of dozens of creatures who cloak themselves in the darkness.

"Care to stick around a little longer?" Malaki says. These are old stomping grounds for him. He lived on Phyllia, Memnos's sister island, but from everything he's told me, he spent most of his time here, running with monsters. "We can head over to Phyllia," he continues, "where the women change faces and the ale never stops flowing."

I'm not much in the mood to linger, nor am I all that interested in ale or women—despite the day's earlier activities.

Malaki nudges me with his arm. "C'mon, Eurion. You're in no shape to be alone."

He's right. If I had it my way, I'd sit in the darkness and think of all the ways I might kill my father.

A low chuckle comes from the dense foliage to my left. "Malaki Phantasia." A creature steps out from the darkness. "It's been a while."

I stare at the hobgoblin, with his pointed nose and pointed chin, and the rows of pointed teeth that fill his mouth.

"Good fellow," Malaki says, approaching the man with a smile. The two of them clasp hands. "I thought you had moved to earth."

"I had." The hobgoblin eyes me. "A witch banished me back here after I ate her familiar." He picks at a tooth.

Malaki shakes his head. "Of all the luck..." The two

men talk, and while they do so, I wander off the cobblestone road, stepping into the thick brush that presses against the pathway. There are things that hide in the wilds here, things that even fairies are scared of.

I don't much care.

I move deeper into the forest. Dark pixies glow deep crimson and violet colors; they perch on branches, watching me. I hear the slick slide of scales over dead leaves and the howl of beasts better left alone.

I've heard so many cautionary tales about staying away from the woods here, but right now I don't have it in me to fear this place.

From where I stand, the stars are all but invisible, cloaked by the dense foliage that greedily feeds off the darkness.

I can almost pretend the canopy above me is the arching ceiling of my cavernous home. And the haunted cries of banshees and wraiths I can almost imagine are my mother's weary sighs.

"She was a brave one, hiding you like that."

My head whips around.

Standing amongst the twisted trees is a beautiful woman, her silver hair hanging in spirals to her waist.

"Your mother," she adds.

I furrow my brows, leaning back just a little. It's not smart to trust the things that dwell in the forests of Memnos. Especially beautiful, dreadful things.

She smirks, picking her way toward me through the underbrush.

"Who are you?" I ask, my eyes flicking over her.

She clucks her tongue. "Desmond Flynn, you know better than most that, if you want answers, you have to first pay."

How does she know my real name?

…*She knows many things*…

She reaches out to cup my cheek. I stare at her, not sure whether I should turn and leave, or linger and hear what she has to say.

She doesn't give me a choice.

I feel a tiny bite of pain as one of her sharp nails slices through the skin above my jaw. I push her hand away just as she presses her thumb against the cut.

She laughs, the sound like bells, as she backs away from me. A few droplets of my blood coat her thumb. She rubs it between her fingers then slides her bloody thumb along her tongue.

"Mmm," she says, briefly closing her eyes. "*That's* unusual."

I breathe in her magic.

Some sort of prophetess.

Her eyes open. "Perhaps I should call you Desmond *Nyx*, heir to the Night throne, the son who should've died."

Instinctively, my hand moves to the dagger at my waist.

Her lips curve. "Was I not supposed to know that?" She presses a finger to her mouth, tapping it twice. "Fine, Eurion Nova, bastard-born whoreson, you are a nobody from nowhere who will do nothing with your life and the slave you're soulmated to. Is that what you want to hear?"

Soulmated to…a slave?

No. Gods' hands, *no.*

"You lie," I say.

The fae woman cocks her head. "About what? Your mother being a whore? Or you being a bastard?"

"I don't have a soul mate." Fae or otherwise.

"Oh, *that.*" Her eyes flick over me and she smiles. "I

57

thought you'd be happy to hear you have a mate. Not all fairies do, you know."

My stomach bottoms out at the possibility. Can a fairy even *be* mated to a human?

She must be lying.

The woman studies me, her pleased expression growing. "So the mighty Desmond Flynn is okay freeing slaves but not marrying one?" She *tsks*. "Awfully hypocritical for the man who was raised powerless and penniless."

I taste a bit of bile at the back of my throat.

"You lie," I repeat, my voice hoarse.

She gives me a pitying look. "Oh my Lord, what that I were."

What this woman says is lunacy.

"I'm not a lord," I respond, swallowing.

I've never even bedded a slave. To take one as my wife, my *soul mate*...

"Right," she says saucily, "you're a bastard. I forget, we're still playing *pretend*."

I watch her as she begins to circle me.

Shit, *could* she be telling the truth? She knew other things about me.

If what she says is true, I've been destined for heartache. Even if I look past how coarse and petty humans can be, there's still their insignificant lifespan to deal with. A mortal life can begin and end within the snap of my fingers.

"Eurion?" Malaki's voice rings out in the night air.

I close my eyes. This moment, which I'd assumed couldn't get any worse, just did.

I glance over my shoulder. Malaki stands several feet behind me, looking between me and the fae woman.

The woman lifts her eyebrows. "Does my Lord have

friends? My, have you come a long way since your humble beginnings. Too bad he doesn't even know your real name. Hard to keep a friendship when it's built on lies."

Malaki steps forward. "Leave us, wench."

She doesn't budge. Instead, she licks the last of my blood off her finger. Her eyelids flutter closed.

"Oh, what future awaits you!" she says, her eyes darting back and forth beneath her lids. All at once, they snap open. "I'd tell you the rest, but where's the fun in living if you already know how it all ends?"

She begins to back away into the foliage. "Son of Galleghar Nyx, you're going to need more than sheer fury to kill your father. Join the royal guard. Find your valor. What you seek lies on the other side of it. Perhaps then a different sort of ruler will reign over the Kingdom of Night.

"Oh, and be kind to your dear human mate. You really don't deserve her."

The prophetess disappears into the trees, and now I'm left with the mess she made.

Several seconds pass in silence.

"Galleghar Nyx…is your father?" Malaki finally says.

Should I flee? Should I kill my closest friend—my brother?

As soon as the thought crosses my mind, I feel shame wash over me. I am not my father, who kills his foes the moment he senses a threat.

Lying always works.

I piece together the excuse I plan to say. The lie already tastes bitter, and I haven't even spoken it.

My eyes meet Malaki's, and I just…can't. Not tonight, on the anniversary of my mother's death. I don't have all that much fight left in me. I'm not even two decades old, and I feel as weary as the ancients.

Rather than answering him, I force my wings into existence, dissolving the enchantment that normally cloaks them. I stretch the taloned tips of them as far as I can, the sinewy flesh brushing nearby trees.

Malaki staggers back, his eyes transfixed on my wings, wings that only the royal bloodline inherits.

"You escaped the Purge?" he asks, his gaze finding mine.

So far.

"My mother and I lived in hiding," I explain. "My father didn't know of my existence until a little over two years ago. He found us a few days before I joined the Brotherhood."

Malaki's eyes spark with understanding. Galleghar visits, mother dies, son flees. It's fairly easy to piece it all together.

"You survived an encounter with the Shadow King?" he says, astounded.

I wet my dry lips and nod.

Malaki swears. "That information could get you killed—it could get me killed."

Or it could make him rich—very, very rich. And men like my brothers...the only thing they love more than their comrades is money.

He rubs his face with a darkly tanned hand. "Gods." He reaches behind him for his holstered dagger.

My power stirs as I stare at Malaki's blade. This is why my mother taught me to keep my secrets to my damn self.

But rather than attacking me, Malaki presses his other hand against the dagger and slices the blade across his cupped palm. Immediately the scent of blood fills the air. The wilds of Memnos seem to still.

Fisting his bleeding hand, Malaki lets the crimson liquid drip onto the ground. He stares at me intensely. "I swear to the Undying Gods that so long as you ask it, your secret will not leave my lips."

The air shimmers with magic, and then it implodes, sucking itself into Malaki's exposed wound and binding him to his oath.

It takes several seconds for me to find my voice.

"Why would you do that?" I finally ask, shocked.

He pulls a kerchief from his pocket and presses it to the wound. "Besides being your friend?" he says, as though that should be enough. He eyes me. "Have you ever considered the fact that you might not be the only person who wants the Night King dead?" Malaki shoves the kerchief into his pants pocket. "The tyrant king hasn't just screwed over your life."

I search Malaki's face, wondering what my father did to earn my friend's ire.

"I'm not going to hand you over to the king, Eurion—or whatever your name really is," he says. "I want you to fulfill that woman's words and kill the Night King—and I want to help."

CHAPTER 5
MAKE WAR, NOT LOVE

239 years ago

***"This is your stupidest idea yet,"** Malaki says as we land in* Somnia.

I fold up my camouflaged wings and look around at the Night Kingdom's capitol.

Malaki grimaces as a Night soldier passes us. "We shake these guys down, we don't join them."

It's true. Over the years, the royal guard has become target practice for the Angels of Small Death. If we're not doing away with them altogether, then we're either buying information out of turncoats or *persuading* it out of loyalists.

"I'm not planning on keeping the king's peace." I say the last word like the farce it is.

Right now the king isn't looking for soldiers willing to burn down villages that harbor traitors. He wants fairies willing to give their lives so that Night can claim a bit more territory.

"What about your face?" Malaki asks.

He means the striking resemblance I bear to the king.

"You never noticed my likeness until you knew who I was," I say, glancing up the street. Fairies bustle along, and they all have a look to them, like they're someone important.

"Yeah, but I'm an unobservant fuck," Malaki says. "These people aren't."

True, there are people here who have seen the king most days of their lives, but the thing is, no one expects me to exist. The common belief is that Galleghar Nyx is the last of his bloodline. And though my father might know of my existence, he has not made that public knowledge.

"What about our tattoos?" Malaki says.

I look heavenward. "Now you're worried about our ink?" Technically, the Angels of Small Death have screwed the king over a time or two, but a sleeve of tattoos is hardly evidence of that.

Malaki makes a noise in the back of his throat. "Honest fae don't sully their skin with tattoos."

I raise my eyebrows. "You've met an honest fae?"

He chuckles. "Aye, you got me there."

We walk up the hill, toward the center of the island.

Towering above the shops is the palace. I frown as I stare up at it, my magic beginning to thrum. Galleghar could be in there right now, prime for killing. Every day I let him live, more fairies die. Some die on the battle-field, fighting a senseless war. Others die because he's taxed the life out of them. And then there are those, like my mother—like me—whose continued existence is an affront to him.

"You sure you want to do this?" Malaki says, breaking me from my reverie.

I incline my head, still scowling. This is the one thing I am sure of these days.

He sighs.

"You don't have to join me," I say.

Malaki lowers his voice. "Because I'm going to let you take on the king by yourself."

I glance over at him. His loyalty can't be bought, yet somehow I've earned it.

My attention drifts away from Malaki when I hear an auctioneer calling out numbers. Ahead of us, a crowd's gathered. Beyond them, standing on a podium, are nearly a dozen chained humans.

I come to a halt at the sight of them. Normally I do something about this. On good days, I simply let my darkness free the slaves' chains. On bad days...the slaveholders pay with their lives.

"Eurion," Malaki warns, using my fake name, "if you do something now, we're going to have to leave."

Freeing slaves *does* draw attention...

I work my jaw and reluctantly I continue up the street. It burns me deep to walk away from the slaves.

I can't save them all.

"We don't have to do this today," Malaki says. "You could free those slaves, flee this place, and travel the realms to look for her." He doesn't need to clarify who he's referring to.

My mortal mate.

"I don't want to fall in love," I say.

At least, not with *her*. A human.

And that's my shame. I hate how fairies treat humans, but I don't want one for my own.

Malaki gives me a disbelieving look. "She's waiting for

you somewhere out there. If you don't search for her, you might never meet her."

That would be for the best.

"When did you become a romantic sot?" I ask, eyeing a cluster of fae women and pretending like I don't give two shits about this conversation.

He shakes his head at me. "You're a fucking idiot. You have a *mate*—"

"A *human* one."

There. I said it. My conscience feels heavier—not lighter—for it.

Malaki draws back. "I thought you of all people wouldn't care about that."

"You thought wrong." Freeing slaves and loving them are two very different things.

He's still staring at me, and I feel the judgment in his look. "You know it's not a big deal," he says. "Plenty of fae used to take humans for husbands and wives back in the old days."

But these aren't the old days.

"That's easy for you to say when you don't have to be with one."

That shuts him up.

I was high and mighty once too—saving slaves from serving terrible masters. I felt quite pleased with myself for my efforts. I was a liberator, a savior. And then I heard that damn prophecy, and it got a bit too personal. It's fine to save slaves as long as you keep them at arm's length. But to bed one—to be *mated* to one...

"If this is about their mortality," Malaki presses, "there's always lilac wine—"

I harden my features. "It's about more than that."

I've spent my entire life trying to prove that I'm more than just a poor, powerless dustback, but I can't seem to crawl out of the hole I came from. Committing myself to a human will once again make me seem weak, vulnerable.

Up ahead I catch sight of the military recruitment center, where fairies can enlist—that is, if they don't get drafted first. Not every Night fae gets called in for active duty, but those that do are often too poor or too weak to afford the spells that will remove their name from the pool of draftees.

It's rare that a fairy will willingly recruit themselves, but that's exactly what Malaki and I are doing.

Join the royal guard. Find your valor. What you seek lies on the other side of it. I can still hear the prophetess's words in my head.

"I didn't leave the Angels to hunt for a mate," I say with finality, closing the subject.

I left to get my revenge, and by gods, I will have it.

CHAPTER 6
ALL PROPHECIES HAVE A PRICE

220 years ago

Being a soldier is a thankless job. The Kingdoms of Day and Night are forever fighting over the Borderlands, the territories that divide our two kingdoms. And so long as they are in dispute, there will always be another battle to fight. That means more bloodshed, more close brushes with death, more giving in to my dark nature.

Since Malaki and I joined the military nearly two decades ago, we've been almost continuously deployed at the Borderlands, first fighting at the territory of Dusk, and now here at Dawn.

Our camp sits on a bit of glittering meteorite the Night Kingdom keeps locked in orbit. This barren landmass makes Arestys look like an oasis.

Only the most important buildings here are solid structures. The rest of the outpost is nothing more than a small city of tents, the fabric of them faded from such extended use. The war has been raging on even longer than the Shadow King has sat on the throne. My grandmother, the king's mother, started it nearly four centuries ago, and it has toiled on ever since.

At the end of today's shift, I head back into my tent, the entrance flapping closed behind me. I sit down on my cot and crack my neck before I reach down and begin to remove my armor.

At this point, wearing the protective gear is a mere formality. There hasn't been any active fighting for almost two weeks, not after we trounced the Day soldiers so completely that they had to retreat. Eventually they'll be back. They're never gone for long.

I unlace my greaves and toss them aside. Then I remove the boiled leather armor encasing my forearms and chest. I only give a passing glance to the blood embedded beneath my nails and between the creases of my knuckles. If I cared much, I'd spell it away. I don't.

This place is beating down my will.

I glance up at the ceiling from where I sit. It's been enchanted to be semitransparent, and through it I can just barely make out the faintest hints of stars amongst the predawn sky. No matter how long I live here, I'll never get used to the sight of the sky, caught somewhere between day and night.

...*Someone's heading your way*...

The shadows are forever goading me, hoping to taste a bit of my power in return for their secrets.

Let them come. I'm in no mood to make idle deals with shadows today.

My tent flaps are thrown aside, and Malaki strides in. "It's our last night on this fucking wasteland. Let's get drunk and celebrate."

It's our last night—for now. I'm under no illusions that either of us will be back in Barbos for long. Just long enough to remember how nice it is to not fight for a stupid cause. And then we'll be called back, just as we have been a dozen times before now. The war is always raging.

My eyes move to the bronze band circling my bicep. I frown at it. How thrilled I'd been to receive it, believing this would be my opening to face the king again. But it had amounted to nothing.

Malaki takes me in, his eyes missing nothing. "You are the only man I know who pouts about a war cuff," he says.

I push off the cot. "I'm not *pouting*."

"You are," Malaki says. "Because leaving this damned rock means you're farther away than ever from seeing your vendetta through."

I push to my feet. "Where are the festivities at?" I ask, ignoring his words. Wine and women go a long way to making everything better, and there's always a little of both around here.

"Dining hall."

Figures. That's where the festivities usually are—unless they're taken outside.

Before I leave with him, I grab a bottle of oil, a dirty rag, and my sheathed sword, my leather belt wrapped tightly around it.

The two of us exit my tent, and I squint against the dawn. The edge of the sun perpetually sits on the horizon.

Malaki and I move across the camp, threading our way between tents. Around us, I can hear several soldiers singing ballads, one even playing a lyre. When we're losing a battle, the songs turn into dirges, but right now, the music is lively and upbeat from our recent win.

Malaki and I enter the dining hall, the place nothing more than a massive tent filled with rough-hewn furniture and soldiers. Fairies sit around the tables, their cheeks ruddy and their mouths loose. It won't be long until the festivities move outside. Get enough liquor into us, and we like to dance and dally under the open sky.

A few soldiers still on duty are serving food at the back of the room. Perched next to them are two barrels—one of distilled spirits and another of ale. Ogre piss tastes better than this stuff, but when you've been far from civilization for this long, it's all practically ambrosia.

Malaki and I make our way to a group of soldiers seated around a circular table, all of them drinking liquor and laughing.

This is how my days go. Wake up, grab a bite from the dining hall, take a shift, get off, grab another meal and share a drink with comrades—perhaps warm myself with a woman—then go to bed. Wake up and it all begins again.

An hour after we enter the dining hall, the room has filled to the brim with rowdy soldiers. I pull out my sword and unstop the vial of oil. Pouring a little onto my rag, I begin to clean my blade, my boots propped up on the table.

Tonight I'm in a grim mood. *Still no closer to killing the king.*

Maybe the prophetess never meant for me to be in the military this long. Perhaps I found my valor long ago without realizing it, and all this time I've spent slaying the enemy has all been in vain.

My sword has barely begun to glisten when the dining hall's tent flaps are thrown open. Two dozen scantily clad men and women file into the room, the lot of them clearly here to trade flesh for the evening. I stiffen when I see some mortals mixed in with the fae.

That's new. There are always fairies coming to these outposts to relieve soldiers of their most *primal* urges, but never humans.

Malaki's eyes are on me. He leans in. "Supposedly the mortals are a gift from the king for our latest victory."

A gift? Marrying a human is outlawed. Even sleeping with one is taboo. They're considered unclean and primitive. To send them to us as a reward…it seems more an insult than a gift.

The group of men and women filter through the room, quickly pairing up with interested soldiers. Malaki and the others around me get up, letting the fairies and humans lead them outside, where they'll dance around the campfires before moving into the clouds for a little privacy.

"Not coming?" Malaki asks when he notices I'm still sitting.

I give a shake of my head, my attention on my sword. So far, I've shrugged off three separate attempts to pull me away.

The girl Malaki's with tugs on his arm with a giggle. He backs up a few steps, wanting to say something, but he chooses not to, instead turning on his heel and leaving with the rest of the soldiers. In a matter of minutes, the majority of the room has cleared out.

Just when I think I might have a little alone time, I hear the soft swish of a woman's skirts heading my way.

…*Slave*…

The woman steps up behind me.

"I don't sleep with humans," I say before she can touch me, not looking up from my blade.

There's a pause, and then her hair brushes mine as she

leans in over my shoulder. "I can promise you that I'll do things your fae lovers won't." Her breath fans against my cheek.

I sheath my sword and take a drink of my ale. "It's not anything personal. I just happen to like my women willing."

She runs a hand across my chest. "What makes you think I'm not?"

I catch her wrist, and I run my thumb over the royal emblem branded onto her skin. The crescent moon looks grotesque when it's made out of raised flesh.

"Tell me," I ask, studying it, "would you be proposition-ing me if you weren't owned by the crown?"

She leans in. "Tell me, would you be sitting here, waiting for battle, if *you* weren't owned by the crown?"

I release the woman's hand and look at her. She has a sharper tongue than some fairies I know, but her features hardly match her mouth. Wide-set eyes, heart-shaped face, and smooth, ivory skin surrounded by wild red hair. It's a very pretty face, a very pretty, innocent-looking face.

"Fair point," I admit.

I stare at her a little longer. She's piqued my curios-ity. Though I've spent years saving mortals, I haven't ever actually stopped to talk to one. And now here I am, surprised that this human woman can actually grab my attention with her words.

Making a decision, I nod to the now empty table I sit at. "Want to join me?"

In response, the mortal begins to sit on my lap.

"No."

I might want to talk to this human woman, but I don't want her touching me. I don't want *any* human woman touching me. None except for…

A cynical smile almost slips out at the half-formed thought; apparently I'm saving myself for my mortal bride. How quaint.

The woman takes a seat across from me and grabs a nearby ale stein that one of the other soldiers abandoned. She trains her gaze on me while she takes a swallow.

"Where are you from?" I ask her, my eyes sharp.

She sets the drink down. "You really want to talk?" She looks surprised.

"If you'd rather not…" I gesture to around the room, where several soldiers still sit. I'm sure someone will take what she's offering.

Her eyes flitter about the room before returning to me. "What do you want to talk about?"

"You're the entertainment. You tell me."

I'm being a dick. I don't care. This is not how I envisioned my last night here.

"Surprising as this might be, I'm not being paid to *talk*," she says.

"You're not being paid at all." Another shitty comment. But it's also the truth.

Her eyes thin. "How was your d—"

"Boring," I interrupt her.

She looks affronted. Fragile human egos.

"How did you become a slave?" I ask.

"I was captured as a baby." So she's a changeling.

"And then?" I ask.

"And then I was raised to please fairies."

…*Lying*…

I narrow my eyes at her. "No you weren't."

She hesitates. "No," she agrees, "I wasn't. My master taught me all sorts of things you're not supposed to teach slaves."

"So how did you end up here?" I ask.

"My master died without releasing me. When her estate went up for auction, I was sold to the crown, and here I am."

She raises an eyebrow at the war band I wear. "A medaled soldier. What did you do to earn it?"

Deep in enemy territory, blinding sunlight burning my eyes. Blood pouring out of my many wounds. Surrounded on all sides. My magic swarms out of me, devouring the enemy and permanently dragging the night into what was previously Day territory.

I take another drink of my ale. "I killed the right people."

She takes in my expression. "So, you've met the king?" she asks.

I stare at my stein. "He was away the night I was medaled." At least, that's what his right hand had said when he, and not the king, presented me with the bronze cuff. More likely than not, Galleghar was either sleeping in with his harem or off killing innocents. It's anyone's guess which he enjoys more.

My hand tightens around my mug at the memory. I'd been so ready to end him. How often does any soldier get that close?

The woman leans back in her seat. "Huh." She stares at her branded skin, "I saw him once." Her eyes flick to me. "He looked an awful lot like you in fact."

Trust a human to notice.

It's all I can do to keep my body loose and languid. "Then he must've been a handsome devil."

She nods slowly, her eyes going distant. "He was. But there was something cruel about him. Something around his eyes and his mouth." She brings her hand up to her jaw, distractedly running her fingers along the edge of it.

"You could tell he was a man who liked killing." She blinks, returning to the present. "Not like you."

I raise an eyebrow. "And what's that supposed to mean?"

Her eyes are far too shrewd. "I've met enough soldiers to figure out which ones like the carnage and which ones simply bear it—or am I wrong about you?"

She isn't, and the fact that a mortal can read me this well has me shaken. Either I have far more work to do on controlling my features, or she's even sharper than I've given her credit for.

Outside the dining hall, the music and laughter quiet. I turn away from the human woman, cocking my head to better listen. It only takes seconds for the shouts to start up.

My chair scrapes as I stand, unsheathing my sword.

"What's going on?" the human woman asks.

Around me, the other soldiers in the dining hall are looking about, sensing something in the air. I feed a little of my magic to the darkness.

...enemy...

...amongst you...

Shit.

"Ambush!" someone outside yells a second later.

Without a backward glance, I storm out of the dining hall. Night soldiers are scrambling around me, grabbing for their weapons. Moving like a wave amongst them are fairies in golden uniforms.

Day soldiers.

I don't have time to grab my armor. All I have is the sword in my hand.

I leap into the air and join the fray, my sword arm swinging as I begin to carve into the enemy. They're everywhere, around us and above us, setting fire to tents and cutting down the unsuspecting Night soldiers.

"*Desmond!*" Malaki's voice comes from somewhere up and to my left.

It's the sound of my true name that draws my attention to him.

I glance toward Malaki just in time to stare at the sun. As I look at it, it dims just enough for me to see the bright gold of a ranking Day soldier's uniform. He's coming at me from above, his weapon already slashing down at me.

There isn't enough time to block the attack. If I do nothing, I'm a dead man. There will be no revenge, no mate, no tomorrow. There will only be what comes next, after fairies die.

Just as I'm about to melt into darkness, a shadow knocks me out of the way.

My wings fold up in surprise, and I tumble through the sky. It takes several seconds to right myself, and when I do, I see something turns my blood cold. Poised where I was moments before is Malaki.

His arm is up, blocking the bulk of the strike with his forearm, but the enemy's blade still cuts through his face, so deep it had to have hit something critical.

For a split second, the world goes quiet.

My friend, my beloved friend. He's protected my secret from the world, and now he's taken a sword for me.

I roar, shattering the silence.

Darkness blasts out of me, devouring my enemies and flooding the dawn with shadows. With effort, I rein my power back inside me before the nearest soldiers can do more than look puzzledly around them. No one knows about the extent of my power.

Malaki's wings fold, and now he's the one falling from the sky. My magic thunders through my veins as I fly toward him. I can barely breathe through the pain in my chest. I close the distance between us and catch him in my arms.

"I've got you, friend," I say.

His face is a mess of blood and pulpy things. One of his eyes is gone; the other is unfocused.

I glance to the sky in time to see the bright Day soldier staring at me stonily. My hands tighten around Malaki.

Very deliberately the soldier turns his back to me and resumes the fight in the air.

He doesn't consider me a threat. His mistake.

I lower Malaki and myself to the ground. My friend needs a healer, but right now even healers are fighting for their lives. The best I can do is take away his pain. I run a hand over his face, feeling his agony throb against my palm before my magic eats through it. It will only last an hour or so. I hope that's long enough.

I look around the burning outpost. Nowhere to hide him. Half of the tents are on fire, and the rest are soon to follow. I settle for laying him across a stack of abandoned belongings sitting on the outskirts of our camp, positioning Malaki to look like he's been struck down. That's the best disguise I can give him.

I move away from him. I have to believe he'll be okay for now.

"I'll be back, my friend," I promise.

Revenge calls first.

I soar into the sky, my eyes scouring the heavens. My fury sings through my veins. Enemy soldiers don't have time to touch me; my darkness snaps out, feasting on them one by one. I'm damning myself by letting my power seep out of me so recklessly, but I've never been so close to losing my friend.

He was willing to die for you.

Only one other person cared about me that intensely, and she *did* die for it.

Below, the world is on fire. Malaki doesn't have much time. This needs to end. One way or another I'll make sure it does.

I spot the luminous Day fairy far in the distance. He makes quick work of Night soldiers; they fall from the sky one by one.

I head toward him, my wings beating like mad. His form pulses with blinding light. He must be a royal. His power is practically pouring out of him.

I reach him just as he rips his sword from the belly of another Night soldier.

My body nearly shakes with the need to charge into the duel. Instead, I come to a stop half a wingspan from the Day soldier.

Control, Desmond.

His blade drips with blood. But as I watch, the blood bubbles and hisses on the metal until it dissolves away. Enchanted to stay perpetually clean.

I take the rest of him in. Tan skin and hair like spun gold. Eyes bluer than topaz. Skin bright like the sun. I've only heard stories of the Soleil twins, but I'm guessing this is one of them.

The Day royal rolls his wrist, his sword whistling as it makes a figure eight in the air. "Back for more, shadow whore?"

I tighten my grip on my own sword.

This fucker nearly killed my dearest friend. He needs to die.

My power is doubling on itself and yearning to break free. But I'm not interested in wiping this fairy out with my magic. I want to take his head the old-fashioned way.

So I wait.

When I make no move to attack him, he sighs, looking off to the horizon and loosening his shoulders, making it plain that it's tedious to deal with foot soldiers like me. Reluctantly he returns his attention to me and makes his move, closing the distance between us. All the while I hover there in the air, waiting.

He swings his weapon, the sword arcing through the air. My arm snaps out, my blade connecting solidly with his. He jerks with surprise. Surely he didn't think I'd be that easy to kill a second time?

He yanks his own blade back, and I let him, still making no offensive move.

He *blinded* Malaki. Should've been me.

That last thought, more than anything, fuels my rage.

Another Day soldier closes in on me. While still staring at the Day royal, I carve my blade up the incoming soldier's chest, splitting him open. With a cry, he falls away.

"Is that supposed to impress me?" the Day royal asks.

I don't answer.

"Can you talk at all?"

When I don't respond, he glances away from me for a split second.

His mistake.

I move in then, swinging my blade. It slices through the skin of his shoulder.

He cries out as blood blooms from the injury, seeping into his gold uniform.

"First rule of battle: don't underestimate your enemy."

With a cry, the Day royal lifts his sword and charges me, and then the two of us are locked in combat.

Left, right, upper cut, downward strike. We're a flurry of movement. Our metal blades sing as they meet, sparks dancing from the power behind each swing. He's impressively good, but he thinks he's better than a common soldier like me. There's nothing like cockiness to get you killed quickly on the battlefield. Death doesn't care whether you were born a king or a beggar.

I meet each stroke of his blade. He should be the better swordsman; I'm sure he has decades of life on me and the best instructors money can buy. But I have my gossiping shadows and my angst and vengeance. That and almost twenty years' worth of constant warring. It's a surprisingly useful mix of factors, and I've single-mindedly used them to master how to fight. After all, I know I'll need more than just magic and cunning to defeat the Shadow King.

Once the Day royal starts breathing hard, I begin to fight him in earnest. His eyes widen for the briefest of moments when he realizes that I've been holding back.

Now I'm the one on the offensive, and he's trying to stop each of my successive blows. My cold, calculating rage has taken over. It's in my every movement. I couldn't stop myself if I tried.

I raise my sword high and bring it down. He deflects my blow, and in the process leaves his stomach exposed, giving me my opening.

I pull my weapon away, and, bringing my sword arm back, I drive it forward, into his gut. It slides cleanly in one side and out the other.

The Day royal's eyes widen. Did he think he was impervious to injury? To death? The way he's looking at me, he must've.

His sword-bearing arm droops as he lets out a choke.

With a slick, wet sound, I pull my weapon out of him.

His hand moves to the wound, his mouth opening and closing. Then his eyes roll back and his wings fold up. He begins to fall from the sky.

I stare down at him as his body tumbles. I should finish him off; all I did was gravely injure him. But the human woman was right; I am not like my father. I hate the art of killing.

So I let him go.

The ambush comes to an end shortly afterward. Once he'd fallen, his troops lost their nerve and retreated, carting him and the other wounded back with them.

I don't bother watching their retreat. Instead, I swoop down to camp. Malaki still lies where I left him, his one good eye closed, his pulse weak. Hauling him into my arms, I sprint to what's left of the healer's tent.

Already there are injured soldiers lining most of the pallets and only a few healers who've trickled in from battle to help the wounded, but the place is not yet swarming with the injured like it will be in another hour. Shortly after I lay Malaki out, a healer comes over to us and begins working on him.

"Will he live?" I ask ten minutes in. Malaki hasn't so much as twitched since we arrived.

The healer nods, not looking up from his work. "Aye, he'll live. The wound looks bad, but the cut is actually quite clean. He'll lose the eye, and he'll carry a scar for the rest of his life, but his mind is intact."

I sag both in relief and defeat. He's going to be scarred and sightless in one eye. Fairies love beauty; having this kind of deformity means that Malaki, who loves women as much as I do, will be seen as undesirable.

"You should go. He needs time to rest." The healer says it nicely enough, but it's less a suggestion and more an order. Injured soldiers are piling up, and the last thing anyone needs are hovering comrades.

Reluctantly, I stand, and it feels like I'm lifting the world up as I do so. Everything is so heavy—my muscles, my bones, my heart, my mind.

"You'll tell me if he gets worse?" I ask.

"Of course," the healer says. It's a lie and we both know it. There are too many patients here to keep track of one man.

"Come back in the morning," he adds. "He'll be better then."

I take a shaky breath and head out of the tent.

"Nova!"

Distracted as I am, I almost don't react to my fake surname.

I glance up at one of the Night generals. She's across the way, but quickly striding over to me.

I stand at attention and touch my fingers to my forehead out of respect.

The fairy waves the action away. "I saw what you did out there," she says.

For a second I think she's talking about my momentary lapse of power, when my darkness had seeped out of me, and I tense. If the right person noticed—say, this shrewd general—they'd know that only a Night fae from the royal bloodline could have such extensive magic.

"I saw the tail end of your duel with the Day soldier," she says, and I relax a little. "You know that wasn't just any Day fae; that was Julios Soleil, one of the king's sons."

I raise my eyebrows. My assumption had been correct. The Day royal was in fact one of the Day King's twin heirs. He'd been the mastermind behind the ambush.

"You are the reason they retreated." She gives me a meaningful look. "I'll make sure the king hears of your valor; your sacrifice will not go unrewarded."

I stare at the general, my heartbeat growing louder and louder with each passing second until it is a drumbeat between my ears.

She means to tell the king. Striking down one of the enemy's sons is big. The kind of big that gets you medaled. The kind of big that allows you to meet the king.

I can feel the wheels of fate turning; after all this time, I'll finally get that meeting with my father. The victory feels hollow. Had I not been so set on revenge, Malaki and I would not be here, and he would've never gotten hurt.

"Thank you," I say, my voice hoarse.

The general nods at me, then takes her leave, heading into the medic tent.

My heart's heavy as I make my way back to my own tent. I pass the dining hall, somewhat surprised to see it intact. I pause, then stride inside, making a beeline for the barrel of spirits.

Five steps in, I stop in my tracks. Several bodies lay scattered on the floor, one is a Day soldier, and three others are Night fae. But it's not the sight of them that closes up my throat.

Lying only a few paces away from me is the gutted body of the human woman I shared a drink with. Her sharp eyes now stare sightlessly at the ceiling, and her mouth hangs loosely open.

I stagger over to a nearby table and fall into one of the chairs, my eyes locked on her.

Malaki's injury might've shaken me, but it's her death that breaks me.

She shouldn't matter. She was just a human, slated to die within a few decades anyway. I didn't know her name, and a day ago, I wouldn't have thought it worth knowing. But she had keen eyes, sharp wit, and a clever tongue, and I had been drawn in by the mind that fueled it all. That she happened to be a magicless mortal seems like such a superfluous detail now that she's gone.

I suck in a shaky breath.

I was wrong. We have *all* been wrong. Humans aren't just slaves to free. They're not the coarse, slow creatures I've been taught to think of them as. If the rest of them are anything like this woman, then they have passion, vivacity, and beguiling minds.

We have let our own shrewdness overlook so much.

I cover my eyes with a hand, and I weep.

For Malaki, for this woman, for this misguided life of mine.

I've been so busy trying to fill the world with my hate that I've left no room for anything else.

Tonight, that changes.

I swear to the Undying Gods that once I'm able to, I will scour the earth for my soul mate. I'll put my past behind me and focus on the future. And when I find her—*if* I find her—I won't waste time fearing what others will think. I'll cherish her, respect her, *love* her.

For all the days of her mortal life, I'll claim her as mine.

CHAPTER 7
TO KILL A KING

220 years ago

The day of reckoning has come.

I can't say how many nights I fantasized about facing my father, but I'm sure that in every one of them, I was more bloodthirsty than I am now.

Today, I'm simply determined.

The royal guards collect me from the waiting room I've been sitting in for the last several hours and lead me across the palace grounds, their faces stoic.

We mount the castle steps, my black leather armor shining dully under the stars, and then I'm passing through the bronze double doors.

I can hear the steady thrum of my pulse like a drumbeat. I'm either walking out of this place with my father's head, or I'm not walking out of here at all.

The closed doors of the throne room loom ahead. The soldiers and I come to a halt in front of them while we wait to be seen. It takes nearly twenty minutes, but eventually I hear the muffled words of the official announcing my presence. A moment later, the doors are thrown open, and I'm escorted in.

I lift my chin. I want to him to see my face. To recognize me after all these years.

The king lounges on his throne, his attention turned to an aid at his side. Behind him, guards line the back wall. Off to either side of the dais are a few of his concubines, recognizable by their immense beauty and sheer outfits, their skin rubbed with gossamer to shimmer under the light.

I get all the way down the aisle, and then the guards that surround me halt. The king still hasn't bothered to look at me.

I bend a knee and bow my head.

I wait another minute before I'm addressed.

"Ah, our victorious soldier," the king finally says, his attention now most certainly on me, "who wounded one of the Day Kingdom's heirs and saved his company from an ambush. Two cuffs for a single act. Impressive."

Even though he hasn't recognized me at this point, I can tell he doesn't like me. Annoyance and even a bit of sarcasm are rolled into his voice. There is probably nothing more peevish to a tyrant than a man who is actually honorable.

Not that I'm that man. But I savor his displeasure, regardless.

"This is not your first war cuff either, I see," he continues.

I feel the weight of that first one on my arm. It represents years of scheming and fighting and hoping. It represents bitter disappointment and a missed opportunity—one that will be rectified today.

"Rise."

Calm washes over me.

I stand, my head the last thing to straighten. For the first time in three decades, my eyes meet my father's.

For a moment, his face is free of all expression. And then, like lightning striking, I see recognition flood his features.

"*You,*" he says. His gaze moves to the men stationed around the room. "Guar—"

Before the word can fully escape his mouth, I release my magic. My shadows blast out of me, darkening the room.

Galleghar's soldiers rush forward, their wings flaring out. The rest of the room scrambles for the exits, shouting in confusion and fear.

I bar the great doors to the throne room, the intricate locks that line its seam clicking as they engage one by one. Then I seal the side exits shut.

The Night King and I stare at each other across the room as my shadows smother the light and the soldiers close in on me, the palace descending into darkness.

The corner of my mouth curls into a smile.

Feast, I command my shadows. In an instant they devour the soldiers caught in their web.

The rest of the fairies in the room are in full blown panic. Men and women are scrambling over one another, their wings materializing as they try to wrench the doors open.

I wait for Galleghar's retaliatory magic to hit me. I'm ready for it; hell, I'll relish the pain. But the attack doesn't come. In one instant the Night King is staring me down, and in the next he's gone, fleeing me just as he did the last time we met.

I dissolve into the darkness, barreling after him. It's almost impossible to sense him at first. The night is nearly infinite and it's full of thousands of creatures. If Galleghar were just another fairy, it would take time to locate him. But then, the king right now isn't another fairy. He's the darkness, just as I am.

I feel a ripple through the night, the power immense and terrifying and so very similar to my own.

There.

I home in on the Night King, who's ahead of me and to my right, and I spirit after him. We shoot through the night, both of us nothing more than shadows ourselves.

How am I supposed to catch my father? Like this, the Shadow King is just as insubstantial as I am. There's nothing of either of us to hold, to break.

Suddenly, his power blasts out, flowing through the darkness. I think it's going to pass right through me, but instead of doing so, it slams into what feels like my chest.

I choke as his power digs into me, forcing my body to coalesce.

That, apparently, is how you make something insubstantial substantial.

I manifest in midair, my body solidifying. All around me the stars twinkle. For a moment I feel like just one more of them—a pinprick of light in the infinite universe.

And then I remember that I'm not the light, I'm the darkness. And right now, my body rigidly locked up, I'm not even the darkness. I'm just a man.

I begin to tumble out of the sky, Galleghar's spell locking up my limbs. I try to dissipate back into the shadows, but I can't.

"Foolish boy," the night air whispers around me, "you thought you could beat me at my own game? I was the night long before you ever were."

His magic has frozen nearly every part of me; I can feel the spell crawling across my skin, slipping through my veins, moving into my very marrow. Every second that passes brings me closer to the ground.

It moves in on my heart, and if I don't stop the dark enchantment now, I won't have to worry about my body cracking against the ground; the spell will freeze my heart before that happens.

There's a part of me that wants to give up, to give in. This life of mine has been a sequence of struggles, one right after the next. So much easier to just give in to the inevitable and die.

The trouble is, when nothing ever comes easy, you get used to the struggle. Sometimes, you even crave it…

I draw up my magic. Even it moves sluggishly. I glance at the ground, only seconds away from smashing into it.

Gritting my teeth, I release my power, forcing it out. For one precious second, nothing happens. Then, all at once, Galleghar's enchantment shatters, dissolving away in my bloodstream. The rest of my power blasts out, shaking the night air.

My wings unfold, and I rapidly pump them. My body lifts back up into the air, my talons gleaming in the moonlight.

Galleghar stops, hovering in the middle of the sky. He stares at my wings, his own splayed out behind him.

"My undoing…" He says this so quietly that I almost miss it.

A split second later, his body dissipates back into the darkness, and once more I dissolve into the night and chase after him, preparing myself for another hit of magic.

It never comes.

Galleghar reappears in one of the royal courtyards, his

body forming in an instant. I join him a second later, the two of us facing off.

After the incident in the throne room, his guards are ready for me. As soon as they catch sight of me and the king in the courtyard, they begin to close in from all sides, throwing binding spells that make the air ripple. Before any of them have a chance to hit me, I unleash my darkness.

My shadows billow and spill out, greedily eating up the guards' spells like food before sweeping over the guards themselves a second later. The soldiers don't even have a chance to scream; the night descends on them, consuming them in seconds. Only their bones and weapons survive the attack, clinking as they hit the ground moments later.

I will my shadows toward Galleghar, but they part around him like a stream around a rock.

My father, who idly watched me kill his soldiers, now narrows his eyes. "If you understood your power better, you'd know that the night doesn't feast on its own."

Galleghar unsheathes the sword at his hip, holding it loosely near his side. Its blade is a dark metal.

Iron. Brave man to be carrying such a weapon around. Most soldiers have nicked themselves with their own blades; it's not a big deal when your sword is made from steel. Iron, though, is pitiless. One accidental cut from *that* sword to Galleghar's own skin would weaken him.

"You want my kingdom?" he says. "You'll never get it."

I bark out a bitter laugh. "You think that's why I'm here?"

He doesn't respond, merely scowls at me.

I pace forward, my hand feeling empty without my sword in it. My weapons were lifted from me before I entered the palace. "I'm here because you killed her. *Eurielle.*"

My mother. It's strange to call her by the name she took first as Galleghar's spy then as his concubine. It makes her somehow bigger and more foreign to me. And she was—she was so many things before she was ever my mother. Spy, maiden, lover, fighter. It took her death for me to learn about all of them.

I move to the outer edge of the courtyard, bending to grab one of the fallen guards' swords from the ground. Thinking me distracted, Galleghar throws a bolt of magic my way. I lift my forearm and grunt as it breaks apart against my vambrace. The military-issued armor I wear is enchanted to defend me against such attacks.

I straighten, shaking off the dull throb in my arm while I palm the sword hilt. "You had to know that wouldn't work."

"It's killed many fairies before," Galleghar says.

I move toward him, loosening my wrist. "Were they all infants? Or just some?"

A muscle in his jaw ticks. The Night King might be an abominable man, but he doesn't like being thought of as such. A dragon that wants to be a knight. How quaint.

My father and I begin to circle each other. Around us, I can hear shouts, and dimly I'm aware that more guards are heading our way. My darkness makes quick work of them.

"You will die for this," Galleghar says. "It'll be slow, and just when you think it's over, you'll be pulled back to the land of the living. I will break you so many times before you die that you won't remember your own name."

I smirk, not bothering to respond.

"Look at how proud you are," he says, taking me in.

I can tell it bothers him, my confidence. How unusual it must be for him to meet someone he cannot scare.

His eyes flick over me, and he sneers. "One would've

91

thought you were already crowned king. But you're not a king. Born to a whore, raised as a bastard, destined to marry a slave."

I almost miss a step.

How does *he* know about my mate?

He smiles, the expression cruel on him. "Oh, I know *all* about the weak Desmond Flynn."

How?

Do the shadows whisper to him as they do me?

I feed the night a bit of magic. *Can he hear you?* I ask.

…cannot understand us…

…not the way you can…

So he didn't learn it from my shadows.

"Tell me," he continues, "I'm curious—did you know that you were destined to mate with one of those stupid swine?"

My grip on my sword tightens, and warm fury threads through me. I force it back. Galleghar wants me angry, he wants me sloppy. He wants me to burn bright like the sun with my fury.

But I am the farthest, iciest reaches of night. I am the impenetrable darkness. Cold, distant, aloof. This man will not be my undoing, *I* will be *his*.

"I almost didn't believe it," he continues. "Not my bloodline. But considering your upbringing,"—he curls his upper lip—"I figure you got more of your mother's traits than mine."

That mother of mine saved me when he'd have me dead. Rather than hate me because I was his, she loved me because I was hers.

"I pray to the gods, you're right," I say. But I fear he's not. When I look into the mirror, it's him I see, not my mother.

Galleghar continues to move around the courtyard, stepping over the bones of some of his fallen guards.

"So all this time you hid yourself in my army," he says. "How bitter you must've been. Fighting for me."

Yes, for a time I was. But no longer.

"It got me an audience with you," I say.

He laughs, the sound so hollow that it rings false. "So you kill me, and then what? You take over my realm? The people will never respect you, a dustback."

Even after everything, this is still what he's concerned with? His stolen kingdom?

Wait a moment.

I halt.

An idea so profound, so utterly life-shaking, hits me. In all this talking, there is something he let slip through.

Galleghar knows about my mate, and now he keeps mentioning my interest in his throne...

He has foreseen the future.

My shadows burgeon, closing in on us from all sides. "You spoke with a prophet and learned the truth," I say, the realization slamming into me. "They saw your death. And they saw me cutting you down."

My undoing. That's what he'd said in the sky.

"Not today, my ill-begotten son." Without warning, Galleghar flings his magic at me.

I clench my jaw as it glances off my armor and shoots into the sky. The next hit follows the first. I do away with it, dropping my sword and throwing a blast of my own magic back at him.

It's raw power pitted against raw power. Our hits shake the earth, whipping about the delicate plants bordering the courtyard and dislodging the pale cobblestones from the ground. Even the stars seem to quake, their light brightening and dimming.

Galleghar spins away from me, lobbing another hit my way, and it's everything I can do to deflect it. The two of us are locked into a deadly dance. I fling a cornucopia of hits at him while dodging his own. I begin to smile even as sweat drips down my face.

Finally, a worthy opponent. One I can unleash my full potential on. If I weren't so eager to kill my father, I'd actually say I was enjoying myself.

I leap into the sky, throwing another blast of magic his way while I attempt to dodge one of his hits. But I underestimated the span of my wings. His power clips the edge of one, punching through the membranous skin.

I hiss, my wing folding up, and I begin to plunge toward the ground as his magic burns through me. My own magic thunders out of me as I fall, and Galleghar doesn't evade it in time. The full force of it slams into his chest, throwing him into a nearby hedge.

In the next instant I hit the ground hard, the stone cracking beneath me. I force myself to rise, even as my body protests. My wings fold behind me as I straighten.

Galleghar groans from where he lies, slow to get up, and I use this to my advantage, pummeling him with one, two, three, four blasts of my power. His body recoils over and over with each hit, jerking about against the shrubbery.

The Night King lies there unmoving, and then, just when I'm beginning to think I finally overpowered him, his body dissolves into the night.

I want to growl in annoyance. Those successive hits should've blown him away; they would've any other enemy. Instead, he still had enough energy to dissipate away from this place.

I've been using everything I have. I'm not sure it's enough. Our power is too alike. You can't drown water with water or burn fire with fire.

If I want to end him, I won't be able to use my magic at all.

I pick up the sword I dropped earlier, looking around me. Galleghar hasn't reformed, but I know he's out here somewhere, waiting to catch me off guard.

He manifests in the air overhead, bearing down on me with his weapon poised. I bring my sword up just in time, clenching my teeth as I hold off all of Galleghar's power and weight.

He must've figured out the same thing I did: that we cannot kill the other with our magic alone. It takes something baser—such as a blade—to do us in.

With a grunt, I eventually throw him off. He tumbles into a roll, getting back up a moment later with his sword bared.

I always imagined my father to be a weakling who liked to hide behind his threats and violence and prestige, but begrudgingly I admit that he's an impressive foe, and not just because of his raw strength. Even though he hasn't visited a battlefield in recent history, he's a skilled fighter.

He thins his eyes at me, then disappears.

I'm moving my sword before he reappears, and it's a good thing too. My blade meets his just as the tip of it nicks my throat.

I'm so close to him I can see every trait I inherited from him. The icy gray eyes, the proud brow and curving lips. I was a fool to think that I could hide in plain sight all these years. I'm nearly his twin. I've been a lucky fucker not to have been found out.

Our blades squeal as I force his away. Before I can surge forward, Galleghar vanishes once more. I only realize he's reformed behind me when I feel the slash of his blade against my back, the iron sizzling my flesh and eating away at my magic. I clench my jaw against the pain, turning to face him. But again, he's gone.

He winks into and out of existence, only lingering long enough to swipe his sword across my skin, and with every hit, I weaken. My clothes soon become a patchwork of scarlet lines. I move slower and my strikes are weaker.

Cannot keep up. The insidious thought slips through my mind.

I might have combat experience, but my father has had centuries to cultivate his power and perfect his fighting skills.

That and he has an iron sword.

I'm no match.

Galleghar must sense my moment of weakness, because he redoubles his efforts, his blade slicing left, right, up, down, whistling through the air with each strike.

With a final blow, he kicks me down to my knees.

I'm a bloody mess. The crimson liquid drips from a dozen different wounds. My magic won't close up even the shallowest of them.

Galleghar walks around me, his face gloating. "This was the best fate could throw at me? A whoreson dustback?"

So tired. More tired than I ever have been.

Sorry, Mother. You'll get no justice after all.

Galleghar spins his sword, a sly smile curving the corner of his lips.

He was a man who liked killing. Not like you. The mortal woman's words ring through my mind.

If I don't finish him, then more women like her will be

bought and sold, used and killed. If I don't finish him, more soldiers will die on the battlefield, more fairies will be taken for his pleasure or executed because they displeased him.

I manage to rally a bit of stubbornness.

Not going to let him kill me.

I get one foot under me.

If I don't defeat him, no one will.

I begin to rise. I'm coated in a sheen of my own sweat, my body trying to purge itself of the toxins that have entered my bloodstream.

He lifts an eyebrow. "Not done yet, are we?"

This is the man who forced my mother into his harem. Who demeaned her to my face, the man who murdered her.

My magic begins to build again.

He's a poison more potent than iron, a scourge that needs to be swept from the land.

With a cry, I launch myself at him, sword bared. No longer am I cold and impassive. I'm not the dark, untouchable night, but the dying star within it. I'm heat and passion, red-hot anger, and I feel so much right now. Every transgression, every slight, every life cut too short by this man. The ruin he's wrought. I'm swifter than I've ever been, my moves more precise and powerful.

His gloating smirk is wiped away as he parries the hits. He tries to disappear, but now I'm the Shadow King's shadow, predicting each one of his moves. The two of us pop in and out of the night, forming long enough to strike out at each other before evanescing into the darkness.

We appear over the bones of one of his guards, Galleghar's sword lifted overhead, ready to cut me down. But in his eagerness, Galleghar leaves his own chest exposed.

I move like the wind, wrapping one of my hands around

his neck. And then, with the other, I drive my sword through his heart. It makes a wet, meaty sound as it enters him.

Galleghar's body jolts at the intrusion. Weakly, his hands wrap around my blade.

No one warns you about this kind of death—the personal kind. How much power you need to put behind your strike to force a blade between ribs. How you can feel your weapon scrape against hard parts and cut cleanly through the softer flesh. How intimate it is when you stare a man in the eye as you take his life from him. It's just as intimate as taking a lover, only different, more terrible desires drive death.

Decades I've plotted and planned and waited for this moment. Finally, that moment is mine.

The Night King begins to laugh.

I look at him, aghast. He took a sword to the heart. The last thing he should be doing is laughing.

"I knew this day would come," he rasps. He sways on his feet before his legs crumble out from beneath him. He falls first to his knees, his hands sliding limply away from my blade. "I tried to prevent it, but you cannot outwit fate."

Galleghar slumps onto his back. He's bent and twisted in a way that only the dying take.

He laughs again, this time weaker as blood begins to coat his lips. "You think you're better than me—I can see it on your face—but you aren't. The need to conquer and kill is in our blood."

I stare down at him stonily. I can feel his words slipping under my skin, and I know they'll eat away at me in the coming years.

Galleghar's head rolls back and forth with his weak chuckles. "We shall see...what other things a soul can be."

Enough.

I twist the sword in his chest. He chokes, his throat gurgling. He grabs my arm as I yank my blade out, his eyes wide, like he didn't expect death after all. A torrent of blood slips from his wound. He squeezes my armor, those icy gray eyes locked on mine. Slowly the darkness leaves them until, eventually, there is no more Galleghar Nyx, just an empty shell.

After four centuries of tyranny, the Shadow King is dead.

CHAPTER 8
A BODY TO CURSE

220 years ago

In the royal crypt beneath my palace, I stare at my father's body. He's laid out on a white stone slab, his body cleaned and dressed. Down here the fae lights glow weakly, making the arched marble walls around us glitter in the low light.

Even in death there's something about his face that's haughty, cruel, unconquerable. From that cold expression alone, one would've thought he'd been the victor of our duel.

I touch my forehead, where my crude bronze circlet sits. I refuse to wear Galleghar's crown or any other, save this one. It's a soldier's crown—simple, unassuming, and most importantly, it doesn't get in the fucking way if battle breaks out.

I've lived too long in the muck to develop a taste for fancy things.

I drop my hand. That last night of Galleghar's life, the night I killed him, he'd known I'd take his kingdom from him. Even I hadn't really grasped that. I'd assumed I could come in, finish him off, and disappear into thin air. Ruling had never been a part of my strategy. But even if I weren't Galleghar's son, killing kings is how conquerors come to power.

So here I am, reluctant to lead, but even more reluctant to abdicate and let one of Galleghar's scheming sycophants inherit the throne.

I walk around my father's body and rub my lower lip with my thumb. I hate that he's here, lingering in this castle even now. I have no intention of letting him stay, but for the moment, there's no other place for him to go.

It's been weeks since I ran him through with my sword, and in all that time his body has failed to decay. The creatures won't eat it—not the hounds, not the birds, not the fish, not even the monsters that live in the wilds of Memnos. Those were my first attempts to dispose of him—much to the shock and horror of all the haughty nobles. They're more frightened of me and my barbaric ways than they ever were of my father.

When the creatures wouldn't consume Galleghar's body, I tried to bury him, only to have the earth spit him back out. I tried to set his body to sea, but the water refused to take him in. Not even fire would desecrate his flesh; the pyre burned to the ground, and once the last dying embers extinguished, Galleghar was still there, every hair on his head intact.

I study him now, my eyes narrowing. There are only three reasons a body fails to decay: One, the fairy is not dead. Two, a fairy is too pure of heart to return to the earth. And three, a fairy is so depraved that nature refuses to claim him.

This last reason sounds the most accurate.

My mouth thins as I look at the incorruptible body of Galleghar Nyx. Far above me, the last women of his harem are packing up their things and leaving. Of his hundreds of concubines—and by the end, there were hundreds—dozens upon dozens mourned his loss, some even going so far as to be openly hostile to me. He killed their children and yet they mourned him. I can't wrap my mind around that.

Their living quarters will be converted into a weapons room, a library, and guest suites. All vestiges of the rooms' previous use will be wiped away. It's the least I can do to honor my mother's memory.

And that's what this all really comes down to: I killed Galleghar because he took the one person I'd ever loved from me. I'd called it justice, but this doesn't feel like justice; my mother is still dead, I'm still alone, and this emptiness inside me is still there.

I give the Shadow King a final look. So many things I still have to say to him. So many ways I still want to hurt him.

I'll never get the chance.

I grab his body and toss him over my shoulder.

No matter. The king is dead, and tonight will be the last night Galleghar Nyx will haunt these halls.

———————

It takes several hours to arrive in the Banished Lands. This barren, craggy wasteland is the one area of the Otherworld that's ruled by none of the main kingdoms. If you committed some great sin and managed to avoid a death sentence, chances are you'll be banished here, which for most fairies is about the same as a death sentence.

An open plain of sunbaked earth stretches out around me, devoid of life. The flat, arid landscape is only broken up by the steep, rocky cliffs that border me on either side.

It's not simply that this place is empty of life. It's that magic itself has been razed from the land.

Most of the Otherworld is steeped in power. It's in the air, the water, the plants, and animals—in the very earth itself. And it's that power that gives us life.

The story behind the Banished Lands is that, long ago, when the pantheon of gods came to rule the Otherworld, Oberon and Titania, the Mother and the Father, were the first to discover magic. It lay in the wild fields and the shining sea. It cast itself wide with the night and blossomed with the dawn of each day.

They found that they could strengthen themselves by drinking deep off the land, and so they did. The Mother and the Father, realizing the hearts of fairies always hungered, sought to temper their fellows' appetites, and so they gave each god domain over one aspect of the Otherworld— night, day, land, sea, plants, animals, love, war, death. On and on the power was sectioned off and bequeathed until all had a little. Each god could draw power from the aspect they ruled, and from it alone. Only Oberon and Titania could draw magic from everything.

But fairies *are* hungry creatures, especially godly ones, and not so long after they were given the gift of magic, many of the lesser gods rose up against Oberon and Titania. A great battle was fought between these titans here in this part of the Otherworld. The gods stole magic from the air, from the earth, from the plants and animals that roamed the land. They pulled it from the streams and spun it from the stars and the shadows. All of this to fuel their monstrous power.

In the end, the Mother and the Father defeated their enemies and slaughtered them where they stood. But the damage had already been done. The land had been so overdrawn of its resources that it became magically barren. No amount of time and no amount of restorative magic could undo the damage.

And so the Banished Lands came to be.

Even the mortal world has more magic than this place. It's every fairy's nightmare. To be cut off from the sustenance that keeps us going...it can drive a fae insane.

Ahead of me, a cluster of rocks marks my destination. I stride to it, my father's body still slumped over my shoulder.

I use my magic to roll away the largest of the boulders. Beneath it, a hole gapes in the earth. I drop down into it, lighting the cavern up with a bit more of my power. The fae lights I cast glow weakly as the land wrings out my magic and dries it up. Everything here takes a little more power for a little less payout.

The subterranean room I enter is nothing more than a pit carved from the earth, and the great king's sarcophagus is merely a boulder crudely carved into a lidded casket. Using my power, I remove the lid, and then I dump my father into the stone coffin.

I can't burn him, bury him, or feed him to scavengers, but I can banish him. I can let him lie where magic dies.

With another flick of my wrist, the lid lifts itself into the air and slides back onto the coffin.

The last thing I see is Galleghar's face, and then the stone lid grinds over it, closing with a deep boom.

One by one, I let the fairy lights wink out. I pause before I leave, a wave of trepidation sliding over me.

Why won't the Otherworld take his body?

It bugs me. Magic defies logic, but even it sticks to certain patterns.

I take one last look at my father's tomb. Then shaking off my foreboding, I disappear into the night.

CHAPTER 9
ALL IS FAIR IN LOVE

208 years ago

It's been almost thirty years, but I'm back in the wilds of Memnos, searching for a prophetess whose name I don't know.

"It's a stupid idea," Malaki said when I told him where I was going. "There are things there that don't give a shit that you're king. They'll eat you all the same."

I slid my daggers into my belt. "Then I'll make them fear me."

He frowned at me.

"I need to talk to that woman," I explained. "She has the answers I seek."

"At least let me go with you," he pleaded.

But I hadn't let him join me. Malaki was the only one I trusted enough to rule in my stead.

So now I wander through the dark forest alone. The place is ominously quiet, save for a few unnatural howls every now and then.

I get the distinct impression that I'm being stalked, but by what, I have no clue.

Let them stalk me, I could use a fight.

"Where is she?" I ask the shadows.

...Who?...

"The prophetess," I say. I cast her image into the night. The darkness gathers around it, studying her features.

"Looking for me?" a voice purrs at my back.

I turn and face the woman herself. She's just as I remembered. Her silver hair cascades to her waist, and her eyes are just a touch mad.

Those mad eyes rake over me. "Desmond Flynn, it has been a while. Tell me, why has my king come to visit?"

Unlike the last time I met with her, it's not a shock to hear my real name spoken from her lips. Now that I'm no longer in hiding—now that I'm king—it's the name I go by.

I thought that I'd want to shake everything about my sad childhood, but I'm oddly sentimental about my name. It's a reminder of my humble beginnings—and the mother who gave up all for me in the end.

"I think you already know," I say. In truth, I'm not sure that the prophetess does. I don't know how omniscient she is. But better to assume the worst.

She raises her eyebrows. "Oh do I now?"

I don't respond.

Her gaze flicks to my war cuffs. "I see you followed my instructions." Her attention floats up to me. "I'm curious," she says, "did you enjoy killing him?" She smiles a little as she asks it.

The prophetess begins to walk around me, her skirts swishing with the movement. "I imagine you did." She touches one of my arms, running her fingers lightly down

107

it. "You had so much anger in your blood the last time we spoke. I wonder if it still burns as hotly…"

I lift a mocking eyebrow. "Is this the best reading you can do these days? It's distinctly *less* impressive than I remembered."

"Ah, the mighty king is finally coming into his own. I'll try my best to meet your expectations." She smiles at me, like she can see right through my bravado.

The prophetess halts in front of me. "So you're not here to end your father, and you already have the crown…" She lifts up her fingers. "Let's see: revenge, power—ah, that leaves *love.*" She looks positively delighted. "You're here about the human girl, aren't you?" She throws her head back and laughs. "The mighty Desmond Flynn has been cut down by love."

This is distinctly unamusing.

She clasps my cheeks in her hands, startling me.

"Say it," she says.

"Say what?"

"Say that you're here for her—the human girl. Say, 'I'm in love with a slave I've never met.'"

Oh, for fuck's sake.

"'I'm in love with a slave I've never met.'"

She laughs again. "Say, 'The thought of her gets my prick hard.'"

I'm dealing with a mad woman. I begin to pull away from her.

"Ah, ah," she chides. Her magic lashes out, slashing open the skin along my neck.

I grab her by the throat as my blood begins to flow, slamming her back against a nearby tree. "You do realize it's high treason to wound the king?" I say softly.

Perhaps I'll get to fight tonight after all.

She reaches out and pats my cheek. "Come, now, Desmond, don't be a poor sport. Prophecies don't come freely." As she speaks, the blood dripping down my neck begins to sizzle away. The prophetess collecting her payment.

Reluctantly, I release the woman.

She rubs her neck, her eyes going distant. "Your human mate is going to drive you half insane before you find her, and even more so once you do."

The prophetess's gaze sharpens once more. She backs away, and I think this is just part of her restless nature until I realize *she's leaving*.

I stride after her. "Wait, that's *it*?"

I touch the healing wound along my neck. I gave her much more of my blood this time than I had before. Surely she has more for me than a single sentence's worth of a prophecy? Especially one that I could've told her myself.

She gives me a puzzled look. "Have I displeased you, my king?" The corner of her mouth curves up just the slightest.

I want to shake this woman. "That wasn't a prophecy," I growl.

"It was," she says, "it just wasn't the one you wanted." She gives me a wry look. "You thought finding her would be easy? That somehow the Fates should go easy on you because her life thread is so much shorter than ours?" She touches my chest, right where my heart rests beneath flesh and cloth. "Love costs even more than power, even more than revenge or hate."

The prophetess drops her hand and backs away. "I do hope you find her. Best of luck, my king," she says, and I think she means it.

With that, she melts into the forest. And I'm no better off than I was before.

CHAPTER 10
ON TO EARTH

174 years ago

I adjust my strange clothes, staring at my reflection in one of the mirrors that line the palace halls. My outfit is far coarser than what I'm used to. I can practically feel the calloused hands and the hours of toil that went into spinning the cloth, then weaving it, then meticulously dyeing it, cutting it, shaping it, sewing it.

It reminds me of a time I'm better off forgetting, a time when I had to pretend I wasn't bursting at my seams with power.

I hear the soft pad of footfalls as someone turns down the corridor.

"Desmond!" a fae woman calls out.

I glance over in time to see Harrowyn, a noblewoman, heading toward me, her cheeks rosy and her lips dewy.

I rub my hand over my mouth. *Never should've bedded the general's daughter.* But in my defense, she should know by now—they should *all* know by now—that I'm not good for more than a night or two of fun. The trouble is, every woman believes she's the one that's different. That she'll be the fairy to break the dastardly King of Night of his bad habits. That she'll wear his crown and carry his kids.

Never going to happen.

I run a hand over the coarse fabric I wear. *Need to stop putting this off.* I don't have time to let Harrowyn down easy. I need to leave now or I won't leave at all, and this is the closest I've come in decades.

Steeling my nerves, I turn on my heel and head toward the back of the palace.

Harrowyn calls out to me again, her voice growing fainter as she realizes that I'm not going to talk to her.

Once a bastard, always a bastard.

I leave the fae woman and the castle behind me, crossing the royal grounds toward the circular portal house that looms ahead of me. I fling my magic at it, and its huge doors swing open. Inside, the air wavers, looking like a mirage. I stare at the portal.

I'm really doing this.

For the first time in years, my heart begins to thunder.

Your mate could have already lived and died. You might never find her.

I hesitate, my own long-buried insecurities nipping at my heels.

A deeper, more primal part of me crushes my insecurities with one simple statement—

I must try.

The need to find my mate has grown over the years, becoming a near-obsessive thought of mine. I've scoured the Otherworld's changelings, looking for the face that will awaken my heart. But I know—have always known—she wouldn't be here in the Otherworld. It's only now that I've grown brave enough—and desperate enough—to finally venture beyond my realm.

I take a deep breath, staring at the wavering air of the portal, and then I step through.

Lands flash by me, worlds turn. I watch it all pass as I move down the ley line. I reach my hand out, and the vortex around me ripples. Snowcapped mountains and blistering deserts zoom by. I stare at it all in wonder until I find the exit I'm looking for.

I step off the ley line, the world snapping into focus. I straighten the hem of my coat as I take a good look around me.

Earth.

I've been here a few times. Never for long, but always long enough.

The land is painted in sad, somber shades of gray, and on the horizon, I can just make out London. I try not to grimace. I can already all but see the tired, desperate faces of its inhabitants, can already smell the manure and human excrement that lines the muddy streets. I can hear the hacking coughs of people living too closely together.

What a miserable place. And here I am, ready to join them.

Because somewhere, some*when*, my bride will be amongst them.

CHAPTER 11
HOW THE BARGAINER CAME TO BE

155 years ago

My booted heel digs into the shape-shifter's neck. Of all of earth's supernaturals, shape-shifters might be the shittiest fuckers out there. This one posed as a mangy street dog to hide from me.

"Aw," I say, cocking my head, "did you think I wouldn't find you?"

All around us the sounds of Calcutta drift in. Unfortunately for the man I'm grinding into the ground, no one's going to stop in this back alley.

"Please—"

"You know what your problem is?" I ask casually, boot still on his neck. "It's that all your kind think you can outwit me." The shadows of this realm are particularly disloyal. It doesn't take much to get them to talk.

I lean down and pull Edgar Worthington's wrist back. One crude, black line is inked into the shape-shifter's forearm.

"You have a debt to pay." This is what I get for giving criminals a loose leash.

"I was going to pay it!" he says, his voice rising with the lie.

"You still *are* going to pay it," I say. "Only now, you have additional interest." On his forearm another black line begins to appear next to the first.

The shape-shifter begins to scream as the mark burns its way onto his skin.

"No—no!"

"Now you're not just going to get me the names of all the soul mates registered in Europe," I said, "you're going to get those recorded in the Americas as well." The House of Keys, the governing body of supernaturals, has a massive archive of them. This is by no means a foolproof plan to find my mate, but it's a start.

He sputters. "I didn't agree to this—"

I twist his arm. "You didn't? Funny, I seem to remember you being all too eager to do my bidding when you wanted money." I move in close to his ear. "This time, I suggest you actually fulfill your end of the bargain, or else you'll find out why I've earned the reputation I have."

With a quick jerk and a little magic, I break his left arm.

For one split second, Edgar's face registers surprise. Then the pain sets in, and he begins to shriek. "You broke my fucking arm!"

"You have three weeks," I say over his cries.

He's sweating and gasping, still looking at his arm, until my words sink in. "Three weeks?" His attention snaps to me. "That's—that's impossible. It'll take months to sail to Europe alone."

"'It's a good thing you're a shape-shifter then. Fly or swim if you have to."

I straighten, releasing him. Smoothing down my shirt, I turn on my heel.

"But my arm's broken!" he cries out after me.

"Not my problem," I say over my shoulder.

Back in the Otherworld, I'm ferocious, but honorable. Here, I'm despicable and lawless. Here, I'm the Bargainer.

CHAPTER 12
THE OPPOSITE OF HOPE

37 years ago

It's been so long. A century ago, I thought coming to earth was a good idea, but perhaps all these years I've been wasting my time.

I try not to think about the possibility that she's already slipped past me, time and space snatching my mate away before she was ever really mine.

I can feel despair creeping in as I head down the ley line, back to my palace, but I know I'll be back to earth again.

How can I not?

The drive to find my mate eats away at me. When I lie down to sleep, it's thoughts of her I close my eyes to. When I take another woman, it's my mate's touch and taste I fantasize about. When I sit at my throne or stare at my bed, it's the empty space next to me I long to fill.

Hunting her has become an addiction. Night after night I come back to earth for her, my heart wearied, worn.

These long years I've grown cynical, but I've never lost my determination.

Once I find her—and I have to believe that I will find her—I won't let her go. I'll cherish her, love her, and eventually, I'll feed her lilac wine. I will make her wholly and completely mine, and I will be hers.

Till darkness dies.

PART II

BE MINE ALWAYS

CHAPTER 13
IT BEGINS

May, 8 years ago

"Bargainer, I would like to make a deal."

The moment I hear that feminine voice float out of the ether, I know there's something different about it. It feels like ambrosia sliding down my throat and lighting me up from the inside out.

Drawn by my curiosity, I manifest inside a chic Los Angeles home. There's blood everywhere, splattered on the walls, the table, the chairs, the floor. It looks as though someone tried to finger paint their kitchen with it.

And right at its epicenter is what used to be a person, lying in a pool of the scarlet liquid.

After a moment, I whistle at the lifeless body. "That is one dead man."

I saunter over to the corpse in question. I see this kind of thing far more often than people would like to believe. Friend or lover gets angry at a comrade and kills them in a fit of passion.

There are very few ways to remedy this sort of fuck up. Luckily for my clients, I'm one of those remedies.

I toe the body.

"Hmm," I say. My client's in luck. "I stand corrected. Mostly dead."

"*What?*" Again that voice runs down my skin like a caress, rousing my magic.

"It will cost you probably more than you're willing to offer," I say, "but I can still revive him."

"I don't want him *alive*," the woman says, aghast.

I turn, my eyes drawn to the creature behind the voice. And then I see her.

I feel like I've been hit by a freight train. It takes a helluva lot of effort to keep my face passive. She's unnaturally beautiful, but I don't believe that has anything to do with my magic rushing up and down my skin.

Tha-thump, tha-thump—tha-thump...tha-thump. My heart slows until it nearly comes to a standstill.

Like a bolt of lightning striking me, I feel a stirring in my chest and my wings to begin to manifest.

Dear gods, could this be...

I take her in all over again. This is no woman. This is a *girl*. A teenage one.

"No," I say.

Hell no.

"No what?" she asks.

"I don't do business with minors." I don't know how I have the wherewithal to respond logically. Devils know my reaction had nothing to do with striking a bargain.

Dear fucking Fates and angels, after all this time...

But shouldn't I feel more than this? The connection soul mates share should snap into place upon meeting.

The fearful exhilaration running through me cools a little. I should not only feel the bond, I should feel *her* through it. All I sense is a tingling in my chest and—

Take her, take what's yours.

And that.

Shiit.

I've heard enough about fae possessiveness to expect this reaction.

Still, there's something not right about this—about *me*.

It's an ambush. Someone's figured your secret out and they've set you up.

I begin to disappear.

"Wait—wait!" The girl reaches for me, her voice panicked, and as she does so, her skin flickers, brightening for the barest of seconds.

The moment the magic pulses through her, I *feel* it. It's almost imperceptible, but for an instant I felt a literal pull on my heartstrings.

The bond.

No, I think, staring at her madly, *no.*

The prophetess said she would be human, and this girl is not human, not wholly. The prophetess said she'd be my mate, but this encounter doesn't feel like the instant connection I've been waiting for.

Strange fuckery is what this is.

Someone must have cursed me; what I'm feeling has to be some sort of dark enchantment cast by an enemy.

After a moment, the girl's luminous skin returns to normal.

My eyes thin. "What are you?" I ask.

...siren...

A siren? *Of course.* The beauty, the bad luck—it all makes sense.

"*Please*," the girl pleads, her skin no longer illuminated from within. "I really need to make a deal."

"Listen," I say, distracted, "I don't make deals with minors. Go to the police." This is the normal spiel I give to underage mortals who call on me. Only this time, I force myself to say the words and play the part. I have to fight the impulse to help her.

"I *can't*," she says, and I notice now just how badly her hand shakes. "Please, help me."

Fuck me, why is this so hard?

...You know why...

You too? I think.

My gaze moves to the girl's face, and the moment I take her in, I know I'm already going to agree to whatever idiot bargain she wants. Even if some enemy of mine orchestrated this meeting. And it's all because of her eyes. I can't look away from them. That old mortal adage that eyes are windows to the soul, is absolutely true; these ones are wounded, so very, very wounded.

Perhaps this isn't a clever ploy. Perhaps she is simply as she appears, and the strange pull I feel has nothing to do with some dark enchantment.

Blood coats her, splattered across her face, speckled down her chest, and clumped in her hair. Her lower lip trembles.

What happened to you, and who do I have to kill to make it right?

The darkness hisses, clamoring around me, divulging all sorts of secrets.

...too late...

...She already beat you to it...

...abused her...

...many years...

124

…many horrors…

…got what was coming to him…

Fury washes over me as the shadows tell me all of their secrets. I take in the half-dead man before me, and I have to fight the very real urge to bash his face in with my boot. My attention returns to the girl.

…mate…

Shut up.

"Who is he?" I ask, feeling all sorts of sinister emotions rising.

She swallows.

"Who. Is. He?" I'm nearly vibrating with anger. I haven't felt this way since my father, and even then, was my anger ever this white hot, this aggressive and fierce?

"My stepfather," she rasps.

My power thickens in my veins.

"Did he deserve it?" I already know the answer, but I can't accept it. If this girl is who I think she is…

You don't know that she's your soul mate. Nothing about this aligns with what you've heard of bonded mates. You could be getting conned.

A tear slips down her cheek, cutting through a smear of blood that mars her face. The sight slices through my fury and skepticism, and stirs what little empathy I have. I've seen a lot of vulnerable people throughout my life, but this is the first time someone's pain felt like my own.

I rub my mouth. *She's a bloody teenager, Desmond. A teenager in a bad place.*

Maybe I am getting conned, maybe I'm not. But she's young and frightened and has death on her hands, and the sight gets to me.

I can't *not* help her.

"*Fine*," I rasp. "I'll help you at"—can't believe I'm doing this—"*no cost*. Just this once." I'm promising myself that more than the girl. "Consider this my pro bono for the century."

Breaking all my godsdamned rules.

She opens her mouth to thank me.

I hold a hand up. "*Don't*."

Just get it over with and get the hell out before you promise the girl more.

I release my magic, letting it sweep through the room. First it burns away the blood, scrubbing every last trace of it from the kitchen. If the police were to investigate this place, the kitchen would come away clean. Even the Politia, the supernatural police force, wouldn't be able to discover a trace of blood, though they might pick up on the faint magical residue my power leaves behind.

Next, I do away with the broken bottle. Normally for jobs like this, I stow away the evidence. I've done this long enough to know that clients love to renege on commitments. Keeping around little damning reminders of their deeds goes a long way to ensuring bad men and women stay honest.

I find now that I don't have it in me to hold this evidence over the girl's head.

Softhearted sucker. Even if she is who I think she is, having some leverage would be the smart thing to do. Instead, I burn it all away.

Once I finish removing the evidence, I focus my attention on the body.

This piece of shit. I can reconstruct this girl's evening well enough from the things left behind. There's a textbook and handwritten notes on the kitchen table. Homework. Sometime between a school assignment and dinner, this girl's life went to hell.

Between the broken bottle and the dead man's neck wound, she must've used the bottle as a weapon, thinking he'd keep his distance. But he didn't, he came at her, so she swung at him, slicing his neck and clipping an artery in the process. And, well, as soon as that happened, it was game over.

This slip of a girl killed a man, and instead of calling the police or the Politia, she called me. The hairs on my arms rise. This is more than serendipity; this is either my death at hand...or it's fate moving through us.

I refocus my attention on the man at my feet.

His features look familiar...

I still.

"Is that who I think it is?"

She doesn't need to answer; I hear it deep in the dark corners of the house.

...*Hugh Anders*...

I let loose a string of curses.

The recently deceased is a respectable seer in some circles and an infamous one in others. No wonder I recognized him; he was a colleague of sorts. Both of us lived off the fortunes of criminals.

This girl just made my pro bono ten times harder.

"Fucking cursed sirens," I say under my breath. "Your bad luck's rubbing off on me."

As soon as the supernatural world realizes Hugh's gone, all sorts of people are going to start poking around and asking unpleasant questions. There are dozens—if not hundreds of Hugh's clients—that are going to come calling with their own cleanup crew, ready to erase any damning clues that could link them to the dead man. It'll be open season on anyone remotely tied to Hugh.

And I'm staring at the person closest to him.

I'm going to have to cash in favors for this. People's lives or their memories are going to have to get wiped. All for a girl with haunted eyes…who may or may not be my mate.

My heart skips a beat.

"Have any relatives?" I ask. It would be too good to be true.

She shakes her head, her arms wrapped around her midsection like she's hugging herself, and I pretend that I'm not having all sorts of strange urges to protect and comfort her.

I curse again. Teenager orphaned, father murdered… This story is beginning to sound familiar.

"How old *are* you?" I ask.

"I'll be sixteen in two weeks."

I relax at her words. I can work with sixteen.

"Finally," I breathe, "*some* good news. Pack your bags. Tomorrow you're moving to the Isle of Man." *Where I can keep tabs on you from afar.*

She looks like I slapped her upside the head. "What? Wait—*tomorrow?*"

"Peel Academy has summer sessions starting in a couple weeks," I say smoothly. I'd already managed to pull some strings to get a cambion, a half-demon, half-human child, enrolled. Peel Academy doesn't particularly like dark creatures gracing their esteemed halls; it always takes a few deals and a lot of arm twisting—both figurative and literal—to register unwanted supernaturals. This girl will be nothing by comparison.

"You're going to attend classes starting then, and you're not going to tell anyone that you killed Hugh fucking Anders." This job was going to be the bane of my existence. Hugh Anders. Of all the rotten luck.

"Unless," I add, "you'd prefer that I leave you here with this mess." Fat chance of that happening. But she doesn't need to know that.

"No—please stay!"

Her desperation is a punch to the gut. I don't know what to do with this feeling that's knotting me up. So foreign.

And I still can't decide whether she's a trap or the real thing.

"I'll deal with the body and the authorities," I say. "If anyone asks, he had a heart attack."

My gaze lingers on the girl. I find I'm hesitant to leave her. She's frightened and shaken, and I want to wipe the fear from her eyes.

I push the thought away. Snapping my fingers, Hugh Anders's body lifts into the air.

"There's something you should know," I say.

"Uh-huh?" Her gaze drifts to the man she killed, and I can see her courage slipping. The last thing I need is for her to break down.

"Eyes on me," I command.

Her attention returns to me, and I can see her physically pulling herself together.

"There's a chance my magic will wear off over time," I say. "I might be powerful, but that pretty little curse all you sirens have hanging over your heads might override even my magic."

It's no secret that misfortune follows sirens, which means my power will undoubtedly erode away. And that means more magic and time spent for no return.

This is how it feels to get worked over.

"What happens if that's the case?" she asks.

I smirk. A siren who doesn't immediately know how to play a few people—now *that* is new.

"Then you best start utilizing your glamour, cherub," I say, taking her in. "You'll be needing it."

―――――――

I manifest in an empty lot a mile away from the girl's house. Now that I'm finally alone, I stop fighting my instinct.

My wings burst into existence behind my back.

I practically choke on my own shock.

That girl...she was—*is*—could be—my mate.

No. For so many reasons, no.

But her voice, her face, her *touch*—and the way my wings reacted, the way my entire body reacted...

No.

But my magic throbs in a way it never has.

I squeeze my temples, closing my eyes to think. But fuck it all, I can't think when I can still see her face perfectly in my mind's eye, her dark eyes haunting me.

She killed her father. My skin pricks. Her present is echoing my past, and it's stirring up all sorts of emotions I don't want to fucking deal with. It's as though someone held a mirror to my face and showed me a glimpse of my troubled teenage years.

And yet...

She's exquisite. Perfect.

But she might not be mine. She's a siren, for Christ's sake; she's meant to bewitch suckers like myself. And that's not taking into account the possibility that someone is using her to get to me.

I rub my chest, where my heart still throbs.

But she could *be yours.* And that possibility is everything.

I try to push the girl's face from my mind, but it won't disappear. She has the same inky black hair as my mother and the same tormented look in her eyes that I used to have.

I look over my shoulder, up toward roughly where I left her. Regardless of who or what she is, she's too young for me to be lurking around. I'll finish this bargain, and that will be the end of it—for the time being.

Now that I know where she is and where she will be for the next two years, I'll keep tabs on her from afar. When she's older, I'll approach her again. Until then, I'll keep my distance.

I run my hands through my hair. My skin feels as though it's electrified, and my heart, my reliably steady heart, is pounding away, feeling everything as though for the first time.

Every second that passes, the surer I am that maybe she might not be a trap after all. That she's not just some girl, but *the* girl.

After all this time, I might've finally found my mate.

CHAPTER 14
HELL TO PAY

I head to George Mayhew's place, a longtime client of mine and one of the best necromancers out there. The man is addicted to pixie dust, and he'll bargain away his services in an instant for his next fix. Unfortunate for him, convenient for me.

I appear in Mayhew's living room. A split second later, Hugh Anders's bloodless corpse manifests as well, landing on his coffee table and scattering a mostly finished box of pizza and toppling a beer.

"Holy shit!" George jerks back on his couch, his game controller flying from his grip. "Hey, what the fuck, man?" he says, catching sight of me.

"Resurrect him," I command, jerking my head to the body.

"Dude, you ruined my dinner."

Like I care.

I glance around his place. George's apartment smells like a pet store, thanks to the rodents he breeds. Necromancy is, at its core, blood magic. It takes lifeblood to bring something back from the dead, and George, like most necromancers, doesn't like cutting himself up for the job when he could cut up a fluffy little creature instead.

"Do you want another supply of dust?" I say. "Resurrect him."

He looks at me obstinately. "I've been calling you for weeks now and you've been ignoring me. Why should I help you now?"

"Fine," I say. I snap my fingers and the body lifts off the table. "I'll find another necromancer."

George stands a little too fast. "Wait-wait-wait." He wipes his greasy hands off on his shirt.

Classy guy.

"How many grams?" he asks. His eyes have a greedy shine to them.

"Enough," I respond.

He runs his tongue along his lower lip, pretending to actually consider it. Finally he nods. "I'll do it," he says.

I gesture to the body. "Then have at it."

George stands, his attention moving to the corpse. One moment he's a junkie, the next, a professional. He circles Hugh Anders, tilting his head as he inspects the dead man.

"Sleek-looking asshole," he comments. "What'd he do to get offed?"

I ignore George's question.

When he realizes I'm not going to answer him, he raises his palms. "All right, man, no questions." He returns to the task at hand. "Beer?" he offers.

I glower at him. He and I both know he's trying my patience.

He shakes his head. "Just trying to be polite."

George lowers himself to his knees, grabbing one of Hugh's arms. "Still warm," he says to himself. He bends the appendage. "And rigor mortis hasn't set in—this is a fresh one. That makes this easy."

He stands, turning off his TV and the game I interrupted. He then heads over to his entertainment system, opening a cupboard situated next to the TV. From it he pulls out little baggies of various herbs, several candles, and a packet of matches. Setting the candles on the floor around the coffee table, he lights them one by one.

After he does so, he flips off the living room lights and heads to his bedroom, returning with a hairy spider cupped in his palm.

I fold my arms and lean against the wall, idly watching the necromancer, my blood simmering. What happened to her…it had been going on for years. My mate had been victimized, and I had no fucking idea. I work my jaw, letting my anger turn cold and hard.

Still holding the spider captive, George begins to sprinkle the herbs around the body, reciting an incantation as he does so. Finally, he takes the spider he holds and, pulling out a pocket knife, slices the creature open.

Normally necromancers need a bigger blood supply, but since Hugh Anders is freshly dead, it only takes a spark of magic to call his spirit back to his body, hence the sacrificial spider.

A moment later, I feel the heat of George's magic rush through the room as he converts the creature's blood into power. The candles around George flicker. Then, all at once, they snuff out.

In the darkness I hear a gasp, then the sounds of heavy breathing.

George's voice rings through the room. "According to the bylaws of the Seven Necromantic Accords, it is my duty to inform you that—"

I flick my hand, muting the necromancer's voice. George clutches his throat, glaring at me.

I stride toward Hugh, my boots clinking against the floor. "You don't know who I am," I say, stepping up to the man. "And you don't know where you are, only that it's not hell." I crouch in front of him. He can't see me in the darkness. "Unfortunately for you, by the time I'm done with you, you'll be begging me to return you there."

I cock my arm back and sock the seer in the face. His head snaps back, out cold.

George stumbles away in shock, making a raspy sound that is his version of a shout. For a man who kills bugs and little rodents for a living, he sure doesn't have an appetite for violence.

I haul the previously dead seer over my shoulder.

What are you doing? George mouths. I've brought him many bodies in the past, but almost always they were people someone else paid me to revive. The necromancer has never seen me go rogue.

I jerk my head, and ten bags of pixie dust manifest out of thin air, each falling onto George's coffee table. "Pleasure doing business with you."

And then Hugh and I are gone.

In the world of monsters, there is still a divide between good and evil. Even the most depraved of us have a code of ethics, a rulebook that allows us to survive. The man in my arms might as well have torched that rule book.

135

The rules are simple: you fuck with innocents, you get blacklisted.

The thought of what he did to my mate... I'm tempted to crush his body inward and pulverize his bones. I hold myself back.

I have something better in store for him.

As soon as Hugh wakes up, he begins to struggle against me, but it's useless. He might have the gift of foresight, but seers cannot see their own futures. He had no fucking clue that one day I'd come knocking.

The idiot must've had his own future read by another seer at some point—all these guys do—but my guess is that his last reading was outdated. When someone gets their future read, it gives them agency to change that future. Hugh probably did change his future, and the ripple effects of that decision led him here, into the arms of yours truly.

I drop Hugh long enough to knock him out again, and then I sling him back over my shoulder. I fly to Memnos, heading through its forests, toward the middle of the island. Creatures shriek and howl at the smell of Hugh's dried blood. Deep in the Land of Nightmares are the Catacombs of Memnos, and at the heart of the catacombs is the Pit, where everything drops off into an abyss. The things that live there make even my blood curdle.

When I reach the Pit, I drop the unconscious Hugh at the rim of it and wait. It doesn't take long. The reaves come first. These sickly, humanoid creatures are the gatekeepers of the place.

"It's a human," one of them says, curling his lip. Mortals just don't have the same lifespan or magical capacity that fae do—at least most don't. It makes playing with them brief and thus less fun.

I can't do anything about his mortality, but, "He's a seer," I say.

They reconsider the man, tilting their heads this way and that. From the giant, gaping maw of the Pit, many different monsters begin to stir, some beginning to let out high-pitched shrieks, others, low, moaning wails. There are even a few haunting cackles. All of the noises echo along the walls of the Pit before the deep trench gobbles up the noise.

"Aye, we'll enjoy him."

That's what I thought.

I back away as creatures begin to climb out of the darkness, creeping ever closer to Hugh Anders, who's now rousing. The calls begin to build on one another; this place is working itself up into a frenzy.

The seer blinks his eyes open, staring around him in confusion.

"I'm coming back in a day," I say. "Short of death, he's yours."

The man, after all, needed to appear to have a heart attack, and for that to happen, I'd need a living man and not a body to work with.

Hugh's eyes become wide and frightened as he takes in the dozens of shadowy creatures closing in on him. He doesn't need to see his future to know he's fucked.

I turn away from the man.

The last thing I hear is Hugh's screams. I smile at the sound.

CHAPTER 15
MY TRUE LOVE

November, 8 years ago

"Bargainer, I'd like…"

I don't even have to hear the full sentence, calling from me from far in the distance, to know who it is.

The sweet dulcimer sound of Callie's voice instantly warms my blood and rouses my power.

My mate needs me.

I am certain now that's precisely what she is. Not some trap set by a scheming adversary, but my mate. My soul sings when I am around her.

I'm becoming an absolutely detestable sap.

I lean closer to my latest client, the slimy Politia officer who's still trying to act brave despite the fact that the guy is considering stiffing me.

"You have two days to get me those files on Llewelyn Baines, just like we originally agreed," I tell him. "Use them wisely."

And then I vanish.

A moment later I materialize in Callie's room. I hate myself a little that my heart pounds like a damn school girl's the moment I'm near her.

My *soul mate*. That realization still knocks the breath out of me.

Her body is curled up on her bed, her back to me. From here I can see that she's rolling her beaded bracelet around and around her wrist. The sight of all those favors she owes me, favors that will keep her in my life for a long time to come, fills me with both guilt and relief. She shouldn't have to owe me anything, and yet I relish the fact that she's already connected to me, albeit through her debts.

The room smells...off, and from what I can see of Callie, she *looks* off—too flushed, too listless.

"What's wrong, cherub?" I ask, forcing my voice to be a little rougher than it wants to be. Look at me, clucking like a nursemaid. This girl is going to be the death of me.

"I'm sick."

Illness? My heart beats a little faster. Fairies can suffer from ailments, but they are almost all magic-borne. Fragile humans are different. Their very environment can sicken them—kill them.

The longer I stare at her body, the more obvious it is that she is, in fact, sick. Her entire body shakes under her blankets, and on her bedside table is a tiny bottle of ibuprofen and an empty glass. It seems to be a paltry defense against whatever is ailing her.

Outside, rain batters against her window, obscuring the campus grounds of Peel Academy.

I stride over to her bedside and, leaning down, press the back of my hand to her sweaty forehead. She's frighteningly hot.

This is normal for a human, I tell myself. But even as I do so, my mind flashes to all those other winters I'd seen on earth and all those other humans who succumbed to such fevers.

Callie stares up at me, looking painfully fatigued. "I'm glad you came," she breathes.

As if I wouldn't. The hounds of hell couldn't stop me. But she doesn't need to know that.

She licks her chapped lips. *She needs water.* I procure a glass of it a second later.

"Thank you," she says weakly. She sits up, and I can tell everything about the movement aches.

The water seems just as useless as the ibuprofen.

I could give her lilac wine. All I'd have to do is pretend it's some magical tonic. She'd drink it, and technically she *would* get better instantly. That, and our bond would complete itself.

I hadn't known when I first met her that our clashing magic prevented me from feeling her the way soul mates usually do. It wasn't until I read up on soul mates a few weeks ago that I realized the magical cord that connected a bonded pair was not fully formed between me and Callie. It was there, I could sense that much, but our connection won't fully form until our power becomes compatible. One sip of lilac wine would take care of that; our bond would lock into place...

You selfish bastard, you'd steal her chances at a normal life.

A horrible sort of frustration stirs through me. I have to just watch this play out.

She takes a shallow sip of the water.

I feel my brows furrow. "Drink more."

Callie is well enough to glower at me. "You don't have to be so bossy. I was planning on it."

Ah, there's that attitude. I could live off it. It curbs the worst of my worries and steadies my uncertain heart.

"Have you eaten?" I ask, looking her over.

She shakes her head. "The dining hall is too far away." And the storm's too bad and she's too sick to make the trek.

I frown at her. No one thought to bring her anything to eat or drink? A flash of anger and protectiveness swell within me.

Safeguard your mate.

Fuck it, tonight I'm going to be that clucking nursemaid.

"What sounds good?" I ask her. I half expect her to say that she has no appetite.

"Soup," she says.

My heart breaks a little at her answer. So she *has* been hungry, but she's been too sick to get herself something to eat.

There's something seriously wrong about that.

In other news, I might be the world's shittiest mate. Can't even take care of my siren until she calls on me.

Fighting my better nature, I brush Callie's hair away from her face. "I'll be right back."

I vanish from her room and head off to a ramen house on the other side of the world. The restaurant happens to make halfway decent soup—if, you know, you like watered-down shit.

Apparently, sick girls do.

Callie eats the ramen in five minutes flat.

"Thanks, Des," she says once she's finished, setting the empty take-out bowl on her bedside table and lying back down. "Both for the soup and for staying with me."

I nod, trying not to act like any of this situation is getting under my skin. "I'm going to have to leave soon."

Liar.

"Can you stay with me?" she asks.

For the rest of the evening, she means. This is her wish, for me to sit by her side through the night.

This is new. I'm used to getting propositioned by frisky fairies, not sick teenage girls who can't keep their eyes open.

And gods, how I want to say yes. I want to drop this farce and be honest with her, but the fact remains that she's a teenager and I'm not.

I shake my head.

"Please."

Stop making deals with me, I want to tell her. I can't resist them. I won't. I crave her too much.

She reaches out and threads her fingers through mine.

I frown at our joined hands.

I can't even brush a kiss along her knuckles, not without opening a can of worms I'm really not ready to deal with. So reluctantly I give Callie her hand back.

"No, cherub."

I see a little bit of hope shrivel up and die in her eyes.

You bastard, your mate has no one else.

Why does everything I do with this girl leave me so damn conflicted? There's no middle ground with the two of us, it's either all or nothing, and the more I toe the line that divides the two, the worse off we both are.

She rearranges herself in her bed, and I practically feel her pull away from me. I nearly growl at myself in frustration.

I use my magic to heat the room up to make her more comfortable; it's the best I can do. A minute later she stops shivering, and several minutes after that, I hear her breathing even out.

Sick girl is out, which means I should go.

Instead, I sit down on the floor next to her bed, my back resting against the edge of her mattress.

What I would give to lie next to her. Even now I can imagine slipping under those covers and tucking her body into mine. It would be worth the heatstroke she'd give me.

Fuck propriety and whoever came up with it. I don't think it's doing either of us much good right now.

Using my magic, I call Callie's colored pencils and a sheet of her computer paper to me, and then I begin drawing out my frustration. The image takes the shape of healthy Callie—how I will her to be.

I'll leave once I finish, I promise myself.

It's no accident that this particular portrait takes me longer to complete than it should. When it's finished, I let it drift onto her computer chair.

Cautiously, I creep to Callie's side, placing my hand against her forehead for the second time this evening. She still feels feverish.

Can't leave now. Not until I get some reassurance that she's getting better rather than worse.

So, using a little of my magic, I mask myself from her. If she woke up this minute, she'd see an empty room. But I'm still here.

Every time her glass of water runs low, I fill it back up. Every time she kicks off her covers, I lower the temperature of the room, and every time she begins to shiver, I heat the place back up. And I make sure there's always a bowl of steaming soup next to her bed.

It's sometime in the deep night, hours after I should've left, when it hits me for the first time—

I love her. Those three words just pop into my head, fully formed.

143

I *love* her.

This isn't some bond-borne magic being shoved down my throat. This isn't even romance. This is love-you-till-your-skin-sags-off-your-bones. Love you till then and beyond. It's not lustful, it's not selfish or petty. It's what has me lingering in Callie's room right now when I should be collecting bargains or ruling my kingdom because I can't stand the thought of her being sick and alone. It's what's made me flee Callie's room every time she gets too close because this emotion is bigger than me—bigger than the night itself—and I want things for her that my presence can't give her, like a chance to be a teenager.

It's loving Callie's heart and mind over her face and body.

I didn't even realize that those three words people throw around so casually were created to explain this deep and unending emotion.

Dear gods, I love her.

CHAPTER 16
A CROWN OF FIREFLIES

December, 8 years ago

The winds off the coast of the Isle of Man whip at me and Callie as we stand at the edge of her campus grounds. Beyond the low wall next to us, the land drops off, and the storm-tossed sea crashes against it over and over again.

Callie glances across the lawn, taking in her peers as they move between Peel Academy's dormitories and the castle proper.

"They can't see us," I say, stepping in close. I have to mask my presence as a precaution. I run in dangerous circles; I can't have an angry client bearing down on Callie because I was spotted with her. "But it wouldn't matter anyway, would it?" I ask.

I've seen the way these little assholes treat her. She's too pretty to blend in, but the students here do a fairly good job pretending she doesn't exist.

She takes a step back. "What's that supposed to mean?"

I move in closer. "Poor Callie." I give her a pout. "Always on the outside, always looking in." I know full well I'm taunting her.

"Tell me, cherub," I continue, "how does someone like you end up being an outcast?" For me, it was obvious. I was thought to be a powerless fae; the Otherworld scorns such creatures. But Callie is fun and engaging. I don't have to be in love with her to know she's the type of girl who should have a flock of friends.

"Why are we even talking about me?" she asks, self-consciously slipping a lock of hair behind her ear.

"Because sometimes you fascinate me."

…more than sometimes…

She swallows, casting her gaze back over the lawn. "It's not them, it's me." Biting the inside of her cheek, she kicks at a tuft of grass. "It's hard pretending to be normal after… you know."

I want to tell her that it's foolish to feel remorse over her stepfather's death, but perhaps that's the fae in me. I haven't lost sleep over killing my own father. Gods know the world is better off without him.

"I think I have to put myself back together before I make friends," she continues. "Real friends."

That bit of honesty levels me. Why the fuck does the world have to be cruel to her? She shouldn't have to suffer because some monster hurt her. That's not how the world should work.

I tilt her chin up, studying her face. If I could, I'd siphon her pain away. But there are things not even my magic can touch.

"How about I make you a queen for a night?" I say.

Before she has a chance to respond, I let my magic loose,

coaxing fireflies from the darkness. One by one they fly over my shoulder, heading straight for a very confused Callie.

The fireflies circle her before landing on her head.

"I have bugs in my hair," she states.

"You have a crown." I grin and lean against the stone wall.

You'll wear a different crown one day…

One of the fireflies slips from her hair, tumbling down her scarf before making its way beneath her shirt.

"*Oh my God!*" Her eyes grow as big as saucers, and it's all I can do not to laugh.

"Naughty bugs," I cluck.

I scoop the insect up, forcing myself to ignore a slew of inappropriate thoughts when my knuckles brush Callie's soft skin. I release the firefly a moment later, and together, the two of us watch it bop and dip its way back into her hair.

Across from me, Callie begins to laugh.

She's going to break me. I fell in love with this woman's darkness, with her pain and vulnerability. That had been enough. But when she laughs—when she laughs, that's when I realize I'm a ruined man.

"Des, are you trying to cheer me up?" she says.

I take Callie's hand. "Let's get out of here. You hungry?" I ask. "Dinner's on me."

"Dinner's *on* you?" she says. "Now that sounds interesting…"

Gods' bones, if I didn't already love her, I would now.

"Cherub, I may make a fairy out of you yet."

CHAPTER 17
A MARKED MAN

January, 7 years ago

Before I even appear in Callie's room, I know something's off. Maybe it's the way her voice wavers when she calls out to me, maybe it's our ephemeral bond, and maybe it's the darkness, whispering secrets that aren't theirs to tell.

But knowing something's off and seeing it are two entirely different things.

Callie sits among a pile of used tissues, her eyes puffy and red.

…a man held her down…

…touched her against her will…

I need to skullfuck someone.

I cross my arms. "Who do I have to hurt?" This, I'm going to enjoy, I can already tell.

She shakes her head, her gaze dropping.

"Give me a name, cherub." I can't give her love—*yet*—but I can give her vengeance.

She wipes her face, then glances up at me. "He's an instructor," she whispers.

Kill him.

The need to destroy human flesh is almost physical. I have to tamp it down because I'm doing this all wrong. I'm too much anger, not enough affection. But instinct is driving me to prove to my mate that she's untouchable because she's mine.

I set those drives aside. *Later*, I promise myself.

So I force myself to stop fantasizing about flaying some human alive and instead sit next to Callie. I pull her into me and close my eyes.

She's right here, in my arms, I tell myself. It helps with the frenzied anger still coiling up inside of me.

But then she begins to truly unleash her grief, her entire body heaving with her cries, and it's breaking my cold, fickle heart.

I will fucking slaughter whoever did this very, very slowly.

I hold her close, and each second that passes fuels my retribution. Eventually her crying tapers off. She pushes away from me, and only reluctantly do I let her go.

Her face is a mess of tears, and my stomach clenches at the sight. Frowning, I wipe them away.

My hands slide across the soft skin of her cheeks until I'm cupping her face.

"Tell me what happened." *I will be your vengeance, cherub.*

She draws in a shaky breath. "His name is Mr. Whitechapel. He—he tried to touch me..."

Whitechapel. Of all the last names, this asshole had to have a sacrosanct one. The world has a sense of humor.

The story pours out of her, her voice too calm and her eyes a little distant, a little empty. It's a frightening expression, like she's drifting away from me. But once Callie's finished, that flush of life snaps back into her features, and she begins crying again.

There is no justice powerful enough to fix what this man did to Callie—just like there's not enough justice to right her stepfather's wrongs—though in the end, after his time in the Pit, he came as close as one can to paying.

I remind myself that this time Callie used her glamour and got away. She bested her instructor. It doesn't erase the trauma, but it's something.

I pull her against me once more, resting my chin on the crown of her head. "Cherub, I'm proud of you using your power like that," I say.

I already knew when I first met her, bloody and desperate, that she wouldn't be some idle victim; she wasn't then and she isn't now.

Beneath me, her body shakes harder.

"Want to know a secret?" I smooth down her hair. "People like him were born to fear people like us," I say. I can sense it even in this moment, when she's at her lowest; her tragedies are hardening her into something stronger, fiercer, *darker*.

"That's a shitty secret," she says against my chest.

I bring my lips to her ear. "It's the truth. Eventually you'll understand. And eventually you'll embrace it."

She will. I'm sure it's hard to see that now, when life seems like it keeps kicking her while she's down, but one day things will change for Callie, just as they did for me.

She continues to cry long, hard sobs that shake her entire body. My clothes are stained with her tears.

I don't know how much time passes before I decide to move us to Callie's bed, still holding her close. Fuck my moral compass; I dare anyone to try to pry me away from this girl.

Softly I begin to hum a lullaby my mother used to sing to me, breathing in my mate's essence as I do so. *I'm here, I've got you*, I want to say. But it's a fickle promise. So instead, I let the melody and my embrace do the talking for me.

It seems to work. First Callie's crying tapers off, and then her breathing evens. When I glance down at her next, she's out cold. Her eyes are still swollen and her cheeks are still blotchy, and I'm pretty sure I couldn't love her more, which only makes the pain and anger inside me more acute.

I wipe away a stray tear with my thumb. I have to go. If I don't, I might do something reckless, like stay the night.

"One day I won't have to leave you," I say softly.

Gingerly I slide out from under her, and then I do something I've never done to another woman—I tuck her in.

Love is...not how I imagined it to be. I never antici-pated these little gestures of kindness that she brings out in me. There's something about them that disturbs me, like I'm losing a bit of my edge.

But then I remember that there's a teacher out there who needs to be taught a lesson, and suddenly, my edge is back.

With one final look at Callie's sleeping form, I slip out of the room and into the night.

Time for vengeance.

It doesn't take long to find Mr. Whitechapel. I lurk in the shadows, watching him as he heads out of a local pub.

Callie's instructor is tall and lanky, his thin brown hair mostly absent from the top of his head. He has a trustworthy look about him—non–threatening. It probably has something to do with his mousy features. Even his magic tastes unassuming and subservient.

His shoes tap against the rain–slicked pavement as he walks down the street, his hands in his pockets. He has no idea the night stalks him.

Halfway down the road he begins to whistle like he doesn't have a care in the world. The fucker scarred my mate earlier today, and he has the gall to whistle.

That's the straw that breaks me.

I manifest in front of him, darkness billowing about me like smoke. He startles, taking a step back. It takes him a second to recover.

"Whoa there," he says, "you scared me."

I stride toward him, making no move to placate his fears, the darkness rushing forward with me. It could consume him in seconds, but that would be too easy an end.

His eyes widen.

Yes, now he realizes that I'm no benign stranger.

He raises his hands. "My wallet is in my back left pocket. Take it, it's yours."

I don't stop stalking toward him. If I gave two fucks about a wallet, it would've disappeared long before now.

When he realizes that he can't just talk it out, he begins to back up.

But it's too late.

I grab him by the throat and shove him against a nearby wall.

"What do you want?" he asks, the first note of fear entering his voice.

To make you bleed.

"Do you believe you're a good person?" I ask.

He chokes rather than answering.

I squeeze his throat tighter, my magic leaking out of me, forcing him to give up the truth even though he barely has air to do so.

"Y—yes, I guess."

I feel my upper lip tick. "Wrong answer."

I release him, letting his body drop to the wet concrete. He sucks in several raspy breaths, then scrambles back, trying to get his feet under him. He doesn't quite manage it; his shaky knees keep folding.

I prowl after him, my heavy boots clinking against the concrete.

"Seriously, what do you want?" he says, his voice high and thin.

"Two words: Callypso. Lillis."

"For the thousandth time, I didn't do anything to her!"

Mr. Whitechapel and I are in an abandoned building in Balti, Moldova. The ground is littered with old plastic wrappers, a few used condoms, and some broken beer bottles. The windows have long since been boarded up, and the only light that trickles in comes from a section of the roof that's caved in. The place smells like urine, vermin, and mildew. Oh, and blood. It's beginning to smell like blood.

Other than a little teenage revelry, this is a forgotten building in the poor section of a city and country most people are not even aware exists. Whitechapel might as well be invisible.

I circle Callie's teacher. "What should I do next? Take a finger or break another bone?"

The man begins to openly weep.

A few of his toes I've already taken. I'm considering threading a string through them and making them into a necklace. Perhaps I'll give it to Callie…

…*too gruesome*…

No one asked you. I swear the shadows only freely talk when I don't want to listen to them.

"Please," Whitechapel weeps.

I'd like to say this is painful to watch. I'd like to say that there's something soft in me that shies away from this, but then I wouldn't be the Night King.

I crouch in front of the teacher. "Are you ready to tell me why you targeted Callypso Lillis?"

He's been denying any wrongdoing up until now.

He takes a few deep breaths. "She liked me." His voice quavers. "She wanted to get to know me better."

My anger roils within me. *She liked me.*

I pull my knife out and flip it in my hand, then grab for his leg. His foot is already bloody.

"I think I should take two toes for that lie," I say, my voice even.

"Wait—wait!"

He begins to scream. It only gets louder as I make good on my threat.

He cries for a long time after that, and I patiently wait it out.

"The truth," I demand once I feel he's ready to talk again. This time I force my magic on him.

He chokes for several seconds, fighting whatever answer he's about to say. Placidly, I watch him struggle.

"She was a loner," he finally says. "I'm not good with women, and I—she…I'm not a bad guy," he pleads. "She would've liked it. She *did* want me."

I almost lose it then. Only my long-practiced control stops me from smashing his face in over and over again until it's nothing more than meaty pulp.

His body slumps as my magic leaves him.

"How many others?" I ask, steadying my rage.

Predators don't just wake up one day with these urges. They grow and build over time.

He looks at me dazedly, sweat dotting his face.

I force my magic on him. "How. Many."

He begins to cry again. "I don't know…"

I move my knife to one of his fingers. "Want me to jog your memory?"

"No—*no*!" He sucks in several thin breaths. "S-seven. Seven others."

I consider castrating him there and then. Seven victims. This is no temporary slip of judgment. This man is a serial rapist. And all his victims, what about them? They have to carry the emotional scars for their entire lives, all so that this fuckface could get his sick jollies on.

Coldly, I break his femur. While he's still screaming, I crush his kneecap.

His shrieks are the sweetest music.

I'm sure Whitechapel studied his victims, I'm sure he identified those individuals who didn't have much family, whose reputations were tarnished, those who were social outcasts.

I'm sure he never imagined that one of his victims would have a nightmare like me on their side.

"Names," I demand.

He lists all seven of them to me. Seven women with dreams and interests. Seven women who were just trying to make it through the hellhole that mortal high school can be.

I circle him, wanting to take him back to the Otherworld with me like I did with Hugh. But a bigger part of me wants Callie to know what happened to him.

"You made a mistake going after Callypso Lillis. And you made a mistake going after those other girls, and you're going to pay for it for the rest of your life, starting now."

He whimpers.

"You're going to sustain eight more injuries, one for each girl. I'm a gentleman, so for each one I'll let you choose whether you'd rather have a bone broken or an appendage sawed off."

The next hour is a blur of screams and injuries. By the time I'm done delivering the wounds, Whitechapel's breathing is shallow and his eyelids are drooping. There's only so much pain a human can endure, and he's getting close to his upper limit for the day.

I wipe off my knife and sheath it.

"You do realize you're at a fork in the road," I tell him. "You have two options: I can either subject you to more of this, or you can turn yourself in—you can confess, repent, and live your life as the law deems fit, or you can live your life as *I* deem it fit. I can already tell you which option is better for you."

So can Whitechapel.

"I'll turn myself in," he whispers.

My eyes move over him. "I'm going to magically bind you to your word. If you break it—hell, if you do anything that displeases me—*I'll know.*"

I don't need to elaborate on that threat. The thickening smell of ammonia lets me know just what Whitechapel thinks of it.

I straighten.

"Who are you?" he whispers.

I stare down at him for a long moment, then I make a decision. My business card forms in my palm, and I flick it at him. It's nearly identical to the one Callie has, only hers listed instructions on how to contact me. This one just has my name and a catchphrase—

Bargainer

Make a deal if you dare

Might as well let the authorities know I was here, doing all their dirty work for them.

I step over Whitechapel's toes, which decorate the floor like wedding rice.

And then I'm gone.

CHAPTER 18
UNDER A PERUVIAN SKY

March, 7 years ago

The Peruvian night sky glitters down on us as Callie and I order dinner at an outdoor café. I'm supposed to be procuring a couple pounds of cursed gold from one of my clients here, and Callie's supposed to be tucked away in her dorm like a good little siren, but neither of us much like doing what we're supposed to.

We only have a couple hours to enjoy ourselves before I need to take her back to Peel Academy. Call me her fairy-fucking-godmother.

"So, when are we going to do that deal?" Callie asks.

The deal I'm blowing off, she means.

I lean back in my seat, one booted foot crossed over my knee as I assess her. She's a little too eager to get involved in the seedy side of my life. "All in good time, cherub."

Callie nods, her eyes drifting across the street; they brighten with interest. I follow her gaze, then nearly groan.

A tourist trap of a shop sits across from us, selling all sorts of brightly colored T-shirts with llamas and *Peru* emblazoned onto them. Stacks of blankets made from Alpaca wool sit outside the shop, right next to a series of carved gourds. A rickety stand of key chains and another of postcards border the shop like sentinels.

And Callie is all for it.

Her interest is interrupted by the waitress, who sets down a plate of *pollo a la brasa* and another of *anticuchos* in front of us. A moment later our drinks come, the amber liquid glistening under the streetlights.

Callie tears her gaze away from the store to take our meals in. She looks a bit reluctant.

I might've ordered for the both of us.

"When have I ever steered you wrong?" I say. I was the one who suggested she get the *pollo a la brasa* and the *chicha*. As far as new and unusual food goes, this is tame.

She guffaws. "Do you seriously want me to answer that?"

In response, I pick up my drink, flashing her a shadow of a smile.

Her skin flashes in response, her siren eager to surface, and then her face heats. It's all so positively delectable.

How very much I enjoy tempting her darker side. And how very much I like witnessing her desire for me, even when I can't and won't act on it.

To cover up her own embarrassment, she picks up her drink and takes a large swallow of it.

A second later she nearly chokes on it.

"Alcohol?" she wheezes.

"Really, cherub, you shouldn't be surprised by this." It's not the first time I've given her spirits.

What can I say, I'm no angel.

"What is it?" she asks, taking another tentative sip.

"*Chicha.*"

She huffs. "And what is '*chicha*'?"

I take a kabob from the plate in front of me, pulling off a bit of meat. "Horse piss."

The girl actually pales.

This human! If I could, I would go back in time and slap my younger self for *lamenting* this fate. Being with her is the most fun I've ever had.

"It's Peruvian beer," I say, my voice conciliatory, "and it's decidedly not made from horse piss."

Callie fingers her glass. "What *is* it made out of?"

"Fermented corn."

"Huh." Callie takes another sip. Then another.

That's my girl.

"And the food?" she asks, her attention turning to her plate.

"Not made from horse piss either."

She looks heavenward. Gods I relish exasperating her. She should know by now that I take particular pleasure in *not* answering her questions.

"That's not what I mea—"

Using my magic, I make her fork scoop up some of the chicken from one of the plates, then levitate it toward her mouth.

"Des!" She looks around us, afraid someone will see a fork successfully fighting the laws of gravity.

Her naivete is another endearing feature of hers. I wouldn't pull a stunt like this without shielding my magic from unwanted eyes.

The prongs of the fork bump her lips, and a bit of the chicken falls off the utensil, landing on her white shirt.

She wrestles the fork away from her mouth. "Oh my God, *fine*, I'll try it already. Stop hustling me."

I kick my heels up on the table, eating a bit of my kabob as she tries the dish.

An hour later, our plates are clean, and Callie has polished off two glasses of *chicha* when we finally leave the restaurant. Her cheeks have a rosy hue to them.

Shit. She's a lightweight.

Definitely taking her home *before* I meet my client. Between her lowered inhibitions, the relentless siren that's been making her skin flicker like a strobe light, and my own protectiveness, mixing business and pleasure right now might be a very bad thing.

She stumbles into me as we leave the restaurant, giggling a little as she tries to right herself.

"Whoops!" she says, her skin flaring to life for the twelve-thousandth time.

Her eyes alight upon the tourist shop across the street.

Fuck me.

She gasps dramatically. "I want to get you something." She's eyeing the tacky shelf of mugs that sit inside the shop.

"Please don't."

"C'mon, Des," she says, grabbing my hand. "I *promise* you're going to like it."

"Do you even know what a promise is?" I ask her ten minutes later, when she heads to the cashier with my "gift." I frown at the lime green shirt tucked under Callie's arm; it has a cartoon llama on it and *Cusco* written beneath.

Buzzed Callie has poor taste in souvenirs.

Salvation, however, comes in the form of an actual llama. I don't know what the hell the owner is thinking, bringing the beast through the streets of Cusco, but even mated, I'm considering kissing the man.

Callie's eyes widen at the sight of the beast, and the shirt slips out from under her arm, falling forgotten to the floor. "It's…a llama."

Sometimes, I just can't handle this girl.

She heads out onto the street, abandoning her quest to find me the perfect souvenir. My normally reserved mate approaches the man and his llama, cooing at the creature.

Ah, be still my heart.

I follow behind her, and in Spanish I ask the man, "Do you mind if my friend pets your llama?"

It's a useless question. Callie is already nose deep in the beast's neck fur.

I slip the man a few bills anyway, and he seems happy enough to let the beautiful teenage girl accost his animal.

"Des, I think llamas might be my new favorite animal," she says.

"I thought tarsiers were." She declared it after the two of us saw the creature on a nature documentary.

Because it has such big eyes, she explained, like that made any sort of sense.

"Nope, definitely llamas." She continues petting the creature, completely oblivious that I only have eyes for her.

Her hair slides haphazardly over her shoulder, and godsdamn, this girl is gorgeous. She has no idea.

Here I am, the Kingdom of Night's most notorious bachelor, trying for the first time in my life to put a little effort into a woman—all without her being aware of my true feelings.

Oh, and that woman happens to be a teenager. Technically an adult one by supernatural law, but still, much, much younger than my near-immortal self.

I'm officially a one-man shit show.

I back away from Callie while she's distracted, grabbing a carved gourd and buying it for her.

For the thousandth time I vow to myself that this is it. No more contact with Callie until she's out of school.

I already know it's a vow I won't keep. The moment this little siren calls out to me or the moment I start to miss her a little too much, I'll be back to get my next fix.

It's times like these that I'm not sure I know what a promise is either.

CHAPTER 19
THE FINAL WISH

May, 7 years ago

Tonight, magic is thick in the air around Peel Academy. It coats my mouth, and if it had a flavor, I would call it young excitement.

Ah, nothing like being on the cusp of youth. Mine was shit, but I have a healthy respect for the age.

Down Callie's hall, girls are squealing, and you could kill a man with the amount of perfume that saturates the air.

"Holy fuck," I say, materializing in Callie's room. "It's a war zone out in your hallway."

I stride over to her window, peering outside. Across the campus, students move about in tuxes and evening gowns, all of them heading toward Peel Castle.

"What's going on tonight?" I ask.

Everyone glitters just a bit brighter under the stars tonight. It's my favorite kind of magic, the kind that is purely organic. No spells needed. If I were back in my own kingdom, it would saturate the night, increasing my own power. As it is, I feel it stir inside me. Human magic and fae magic are not terribly compatible, but there's enough of it in the air that it affects my own power.

"May Day Ball," Callie says.

There's something in her voice that has me turning to her. She sits at her computer chair in boxers and a frayed T-shirt, half her hair in a topknot.

"Why aren't you getting ready?" I ask.

"I'm not going." She pulls her legs up to her chest.

"You're not going?"

She's trying hard to keep her face neutral. "No one's asked me."

I want to laugh. I never asked her to bargain with me, or spend her evenings with me, or weasel her way into my life and heart, but she still did all those things.

"Since when do you wait for permission?" I ask. "And also, how is that possible?"

I mean, teenage guys think with their eyes and their dicks, and Callie is beautiful the same way the sun is bright. She burns with such exquisite intensity it sometimes hurts to look at her.

"How is what possible?" She stares at her knees.

"That no one's asked you."

She lifts a shoulder. "I thought it was your job to understand people's motives."

I fold my arms. I want to slap myself upside the head. For all my understanding of people's motives, it's taken me until now to realize what *I've* missed.

Despite Callie's uniqueness, she's still a teenage girl. She wants to be carted to some dance and swept off her feet. She wants one godsdamn day to show all her peers that she is so much more than they assumed.

She wants us to be real, if only for a night.

I can give her that.

"What?" she asks, seeing me staring.

This is a bad idea. A high school dance means rubbing elbows with lots and lots of teenagers. It means exposure. But I want her to be happy. Always happy.

"Do you want to go to the May Day Ball?" I ask.

"I don't see how that matters."

That's what she says, but now that I'm looking for it, there's a whole slew of subtext there. She wants to go, even though she doesn't think she's a normal girl who has normal dreams.

"It does matter," I say. "Now, do you?"

Her lips part, but she can't say that this is exactly what she wants.

My sweet siren.

I close the distance between us and kneel. My wings ache with the need to reveal themselves. Each day it gets harder to keep them hidden, and tonight is the worst night yet.

Going to blow my cover.

Right now it doesn't matter. Callie's eyes are huge, and I love this. I take her hand in mine.

I begin to smile. "Would you, Callypso Lillis, take me to the May Day Ball?"

I procure a gown for Callie, since she has nothing, and then I leave her for a little over an hour so she can get ready. Knowing what I do about women, it's not nearly enough time for primping, but that's all the time she has if we want to get to the dance at a reasonable hour.

When I return, I knock on her door. From here on out, I'm playing it as any normal date would.

In the hallway, some of the girls startle when they see me standing outside Callie's door, my hands in my pocket. Their eyes move over me, then between me and the room I'm lingering outside of. I've visited Callie often enough to know these tittering idiots aren't friends with her.

The door in front of me swings open, and all thoughts of Callie's floormates vanish.

Holy shit.

Callie's loose hair falls in waves down her back and her haunting eyes seem to be backlit. I've never been jealous of a dress before, but right about now I am. Her gown caresses every one of her curves.

I made a mistake, a grave, terrible mistake. In that gown, Callie doesn't look like a teenager, she looks like my queen.

The urge to claim her rises in me. *She's yours. Now and always.*

Give her the wine. Cross over. Show her exactly what it means to be your mate.

I squash the thoughts as soon as they roll through my head.

This evening might kill me.

Callie's gaze dips and she fidgets with her dress, looking both pleased and embarrassed to be wearing it. "You didn't have to do this, you know."

"Cherub, have you ever known me to do things I don't want to?"

"How about my first wish?" she says.

Blood-soaked kitchen, bloodstained girl, dead monster at her feet.

I give her the side eye. "That doesn't count."

"Why?" she asks, and there's so much weight on that one word.

Because I never actually minded.

I cock my head. "Is it just me, or are you particularly persistent with the questions tonight?"

She gives me a playful shove, smiling wryly. After a moment, her features sober, and Callie's heart is in her eyes. She looks at me like I'm her own personal salvation. Sweet thing, hasn't she figured out by now that, though I rule the heavens, I'm hell wrapped in a man?

I give her my arm, and the two of us leave her room. We head out of the girls' dorms and across the grassy lawn that separates Peel Academy's living quarters from the castle proper.

Around us, couples mill about, the boys looking mostly stiff and uncomfortable in their suits and the girls preening in their brightly colored gowns.

Amongst them, my mate is in a league of her own. She's ethereal and untouchable, and it makes my knees weak just staring at her. I'm not alone. For all of Callie's insecurities, she's collecting stares more than she has beads.

My wings itch to reveal themselves. Even these meager adolescents are enough to set off my possessive instinct.

Those who aren't assessing Callie are eyeing me. There's a reason I've taken pains to mask myself when I've visited my siren. The Politia will be up my ass—and anyone connected to me—in days the moment they realize I'm here. I've been on their Most Wanted list for years. The second they catch wind that I waltzed around Peel Academy, they're all going to blow their loads. Capturing me would be career-making.

And that would mean that they'd all come down on Callie, the girl I took to the dance. The same girl who

I've since learned harbors an acute fear of the supernatural authorities.

Can't happen. I won't let it.

So, without letting my mate know, my magic creates the most subtle of illusions. My ears round, and my fae features soften to something more mortal. To everyone but Callie, I'm Des in human form.

Tonight, she gets a normal evening. One where her date isn't a wanted criminal, one where she's not some outcast. Tonight we're as we should be, two flames in the darkness, and all these people are the moths that bask in our light.

Tonight the world is as it should be. Tomorrow life will go back to the fucked-up charade it usually is.

———————

The dance is all fine and dandy for about two-point-five seconds. Then Callie's peers descend on her like flies to a carcass. Fake friends, fake enthusiasm, fake smiles. If I wanted deception, I'd waltz my way into one of the fae palaces. And if Callie wanted to spend her evening talking to these people, she'd have come here with them.

"Clarice, this is...*Dean*," Callie says, introducing me to yet another classmate using the fake name I offered up earlier in the night.

Is this the fifth person I've met, or the sixth? For a girl who has no friends, Callie has an awful lot of acquaintances...

Clarice is looking at me the way the last several girls have been, the same way that Somnia's noblewomen always have. Like they wish to conquer and be conquered by me.

It's annoying coming from fae women; it's beneath my notice coming from human girls that aren't my mate.

"Dean, this is—"

Social hour, I've decided, is over.

I take Callie's hand without preamble, pulling her away from her "friends," who think they can get some sort of contact high on our relationship by getting close enough to us.

Our relationship. My back tingles where my wing roots are. Shit, it's frightening how easily I could get used to that phrase.

"Where are we going?" Callie asks, trailing behind me.

"Dance floor." There I can hold Callie close and pretend for a night that we are everything that I've denied myself.

Couples part when they take the two of us in. Even here amongst budding supernaturals, we're a species apart.

Callie catches up to my side. "That was insanity back there," she says, referring to the students who decided at the eleventh hour that she might actually be worth getting to know.

Screw this place.

"That was hellacious," I say, "and I'm used to events like this." Fairies are duplicitous bastards, one moment ingratiating themselves to you, the next trying to ruin your life. These kids would give even them a run for their money. "Thank fuck I never went to high school."

I step onto the dance floor, the twinkling candlelight dappling us. This is my kingdom—sweat and dancing, alcohol and adrenaline-spiked decisions. Even though I don't rule over humans, the magic thickening the air zings along my skin, drawing my most feral side closer and closer to the surface.

"You never went to high school?" Callie asks.

The smell of Arestys' cloistered caves, the sound of clashing swords as I cut through my enemy, the look on my father's face when I killed him—

"My upbringing was a little more unconventional," I say.

The song blasting around us ends, and the melody that follows is sweetly slow and painfully human. It's so unlike the music of the Otherworld. There, our songs are a driving force, they spin spells and move magic.

In an instant, Callie's eyes are large and panicked as she listens to the love song. I almost smile at the sight.

I place my hand on the small of her back, her bare skin warm against mine. She stands stiffly in my arms, afraid to move.

"Put your arms around my neck," I tell her gently.

It takes her nearly an eternity to do so, and I feel every second of it. But the moment her fingertips brush the nape of my neck, I can feel myself slipping, my fae urges spurred by the feel of her.

She flashes me a nervous smile, and I am the wolf about to gobble up Red Riding Hood.

My mate is ripe for the taking, and this is a night for carting away brides.

I shut the thought down, and all that's left is the throb of my heart in my chest.

"Relax, cherub." I stroke the skin of her back.

My chest burns fiercely as I feel her body against mine.

Love. This is love.

It's being bewitched by the curve of her lips and the way the light makes her eyes glitter. It's enjoying her vulnerability because only Callie could spend a hundred nights with me and still be unsure about my feelings for her. It's wanting to buy her a cup of coffee and some macarons just to see her smile or making her homework dance around her desk so I can hear her laugh. It's all those nights I fled her room because I was afraid of her seeing me just as she has every other man in her life. It's holding her close when she cries because her pain is my own and the world won't be right until it's gone. And it's being absolutely certain that things cannot go on like this for another year.

I can't continue being just her friend. Truth be told, for the last several months, I haven't *been* just her friend. I've let us become something more, and I never should've. Callie deserves to live the rest of her high school years getting hounded by idiot boys. She deserves some semblance of normalcy, and she's never going to get that with me.

Honorable as my intentions might be, I'm no saint. It's not in my nature to keep my mate at arm's length. I'm a fairy; I take what I want when I want it. I encourage debauchery, sex, and romance, and right now Callie is all my worst vices rolled into one.

She furrows her brows. "What's wrong?"

I stare down at her. "Everything, cherub," I say. "Everything."

———

The rest of the evening falls somewhere between pleasure and pain. By the time we leave the dance, Callie's cheeks are flushed, and a sheen of sweat coats her skin.

I'm having very inappropriate thoughts about precisely how I'd make use of that sweat.

She limps out of Peel Academy's makeshift ballroom, kicking off her heels a minute later. Her feet are red and angry, and I can see several blisters forming.

And the big bad Bargainer had no idea she had aching feet. Smooth.

Without a moment's hesitation, I scoop Callie up and throw her over my shoulder.

"De—Dean!" she squeals, squirming in my arms as I carry her down her school's hallway and out the door.

"Don't act like you weren't angling for this moment the whole night," I say, winking at a nearby student who overheard us. The girl blushes and ducks her head.

"I wasn't!" Callie declares, mortified.

I suppress the urge to press her in closer. The truth is, I'm enjoying having her body cradled so close to mine.

She tugs on my hair. "You can put me down."

"And what will you give me in return?"

She lets out a long-suffering sigh. "Does everything have to be a bargain with you?"

"Is the night dark?" I respond, marching us across the lawn and back to her dormitory.

My blood is steeped in an evening's worth of magic. It's crawling through my veins, turning my thoughts nefarious.

I could simply fly us to the nearest ley line. From there it would take seconds to return to the Otherworld. She could live there with me, far from posturing peers and bad memories.

I could be hers and she could be mine.

My wings begin to manifest, and I have to smother my thoughts.

Get control of yourself, Flynn.

"Are the stars the same where you're from?" Callie asks.

I peer over my shoulder at her only to see she's craning her neck to gaze at the night sky. Most of the time, the Isle of Man is steeped in fog—especially along the coast, which is exactly where Peel Academy is situated. Tonight, however, the sky is clear and the stars twinkle far above us.

I shake my head. "No, they're different."

"Why?" she asks languidly.

173

"Why not?" I respond.

That earns me an amused smile. "One day you're going to give me straight answers." She says it with such surety that I should be worried. Magic lives in words just as much as it does in anything else. Believe in something hard enough and you'll manifest it.

The possibility that I might share my secrets with my mate one day is frightening...frightening and electrifying.

After a few more protests from Callie, I set her down, and the two of us walk back to her dorm room. I disappear only long enough to get past the poor sap manning the girls' dorm lobby who has to stop anything with a penis from getting past the front desk.

Right now Callie's dormitory floor might as well be a ghost town. The place is utterly abandoned. The only thing left of its prior occupants is the makeup strewn along the communal bathroom counters and the putrid smell of too many clashing perfumes.

Next to me, it's clear that Callie doesn't give two shits about the fact that the people she's lived alongside for the past year are having fun somewhere without her. No, she looks pretty content just being by my side.

Callie pulls out her key and opens her door, heading inside her room.

I hesitate behind her. My body is still pulsating with this realm's magic. I might as well have consumed a gallon of the Otherworld's strongest spirits; the effect is nearly the same. Selfish, greedy, *fae* thoughts are pressing in on me. If I stay, I'm going to do something regrettable.

Leave her here. Tell her you need to go and flee this place before it's too late.

Callie turns to me, every single inch of her chipping

away a bit more of my resolve. She grabs my hand and pulls me inside, not giving me a choice.

Once the two of us are alone in her room, she reverts back to shy Callie.

She smooths her hands down her dress, and it's taking all of my willpower not to stare everywhere those hands touch.

"Thank you," she says to her swollen, grass-stained feet. "Tonight was…wonderful."

She's cutting me to the core. Here I am trying to keep my hands off her, and she's thanking me for the evening.

Cling to your humanity, Desmond!

I run my hands through my hair as impulses I thought I'd conquered centuries ago now tug at me.

My humanity is the white rabbit, and I'm chasing it farther and farther down the hole…

"Is something wrong?" Callie asks, and she sounds so damn vulnerable.

Leave! Now, before it's too late.

I drop my hands. "I can't do this anymore."

My control is slipping, slipping—

I glance up at her.

Slipping.

"Des? What are you talking about?" she asks.

Gone.

Claim your bride. Make her drink lilac wine so she may never be human again.

"Give me one good reason why I shouldn't take you away from here tonight," I say. "Right now." It's satisfying to finally give in to temptation. And how long I've held out.

"Take me away?" Callie looks at me quizzically. "Do you have another bargain tonight?"

I begin to circle her. She's a mouse, and I'm a cat

come to play. "I would take you away and never release you. My sweet little siren." I run a hand along the exposed skin of her back. Gods, I want to touch more. As her mate, I *will* touch more. Nothing will satisfy me until that happens, *nothing*.

"You don't belong here," I say hypnotically, "and both my patience and my humanity grow thin."

Take her. Claim her. Make her yours.

"I could make you do so many things—so many, many things," I say, my voice dropping low.

I can see it now. Her body beneath mine, her legs wrapped around me. Already I can imagine driving myself into her, her body cleaved to me. On and on it would go, one position more creative than the last. I'd make love to her until she'd forget everything, save me.

"You would enjoy them all," I continue, "that I promise you. You would enjoy them, and so would I."

I need her. On my throne and in my bed. Next to me always and forever. I need it more than air to breathe, and I'm going to have it.

The magic I've gathered throughout the evening now begins to release. It's too ephemeral to be a spell, but it's now in the air between us, luring her closer.

She glances at her bracelet. She must feel it.

This is what happens when darkness comes out to play.

"We could start tonight," I say. "I don't think I can bear another year. And I don't think you can either."

Take. Claim. Keep.

She catches my hand as I stalk around her. "Des, what are you talking about?"

I hold our clasped hands up between us, my eyes moving from them to my siren's face. A face born to bring men to their knees. Dangerous, dangerous creature. I want her so badly I nearly shake from it.

Her deep, haunted eyes search mine. To take that wounded sheen away! I won't rest until I've banished it from her features.

I smile at her. "How would you like to begin repayment tonight?"

Take—claim—keep.

"Desmond Flynn, whatever's going on, I need you to snap out of it."

Her voice drags me from the darkness.

I can feel Callie's hand trembling just the slightest. At best she's apprehensive of me; at worst, I've frightened her.

What am I doing? Tonight was supposed to be about her, not me.

I bring her hand to my lips, closing my eyes as I do so. My fae inclinations batter at me. It's all I can do to stand there and ride through the urges that want to take over.

At some point, the almost painful need to cart Callie off finally retreats, leaving me exhausted. My muscles ache; even my bones are weary.

I open my eyes.

"I'm sorry, cherub," I say hoarsely. "You weren't meant to see that." Centuries of control—all gone in a single instant. "I am...not human, for all I appear to be."

Callie steps closer to me, and it's the last thing I expect.

She tilts her head. "Do you...like me?" she asks.

Shit. Now's not a good time to have this conversation, not when the urge to claim her is skewering me.

I release her hand. "*Callie.*" I say her name the same way I'd say *stop*.

Need to leave.

"Do you?" she presses.

Of course I do, cherub. To anyone else it would've been painfully obvious. But not my Callie, who believes love is something she only gets to window shop.

I brush my thumb against her cheekbone, wanting her so desperately. I'm so damn tired of fighting myself, denying these feelings, pushing her away.

So for once, I don't.

I bow my head in a nod.

Callie's skin brightens at my confession, she and her siren clearly thrilled. She rises to her tiptoes, her eyelids dropping low, her lips parting.

"Callie—"

Before I finish protesting, she presses her mouth to mine.

Ye gods! It's demanding all of my restraint to keep my own lips immobile against hers. Even so, the world explodes in a kaleidoscope of color and magic.

Reflexively I reach up, my hands encircling her upper arms. I squeeze them, wanting to drag her closer and part her sweet lips so I can discover exactly what Callie tastes like.

My mouth was made to kiss hers.

Useless to fight this, like trying to make a stand against a hurricane. With a groan, the last of my battered self-restraint gives. It bent me until I broke. Now all I can do is let it sweep me away.

I enfold her in my arms, my mouth moving hungrily over hers.

Better than my wildest imaginings.

The kiss is nothing more than a taste of passion, and yet it redefines everything. I've enjoyed thousands of kisses over my lifetime, but this is the one that ruins me for all others.

Knowing that I shouldn't be savoring these lips only makes me all the more consumed by them.

Callie's arms encircle me. A hundred times I'd imagined this moment. All my imaginings pale to the reality of it.

I move one of my hands to her hair, my fingers delving into her rich locks. I need her closer.

Callie pulls away to draw in air—

What in seven hells are you doing, you fool? The sobering thought cuts through my passion and my raging instincts.

Fucking fuck.

All at once I drop my hold on her and stagger back. Callie coats my lips, and all I want is more.

No. No more.

The shadows around me churn as I fight myself. They reach for Callie, wanting to shroud her in my magic.

Claim—keep!

My wings punch through my magic. They spread wide behind me, forcing me to recognize my mate.

She is *mine*.

Her eyes widen. "Your wings…"

My little secret is out.

All my plans—to bide my time, to learn her ways and be her companion for another year—all gone in an instant. There will be no slow burn wooing her; we're a lit fuse, and this situation is going to explode any second now.

I'll either need to backpedal my way out of this or rush my young mate into a relationship she might not be ready for.

"I'm sorry," I say. Impossible, this situation I've created for us. "It was never supposed to happen like this. I should've waited. I'd intended to wait."

"Des, what's wrong?" Callie moves toward me.

I run a hand through my hair. Should've known it would end like this. Should've realized how close I already was to caving to my urges.

"I have to go."

"No," she says, her skin losing its luminescence.

I can see her heart breaking in front of me, and for the millionth time in my life I wonder if being honorable is doing us more damage than good.

But she needs to see what honor looks like on a man. I'm the last person to advocate for it—truly, I am—but for once in my life, I'm trying not to be a selfish bastard.

"I'm sorry," I repeat, my resolve hardening. "I meant to give you more time. I never should have done this—any of it."

Her face falls.

Really fucking need to leave. I'm going to cave again if I stay.

"But you *like* me," she insists.

What I would give for the world to be that simple. If I could act on my emotions the way she seems to think I can, I'd have mated and crowned her months ago. Hell, the two of us would be ruling my kingdom from my bed.

Only that's not the way the world works. Callie still has to enjoy her youth and discover herself. She's been so desperate for my company, and I've been too weak to deny her it, that neither of us have given her a chance to figure out who exactly Callypso Lillis is under all that pain and beauty.

"I'm a king, Callie," I try to reason with her. "And you're…"

Mine. Take her. Mine.

I force the thought away.

"Innocent," I finish.

"I'm not innocent," she insists.

I move to her and cup her cheek. She might still have shadows in her eyes, but she hasn't lost her vivacity for life. She hasn't become cynical. Not like me, and not like most of the world.

"You are," I insist. "You are so painfully innocent in so many ways, and I'm a very, very bad man. You should stay away from me because I can't seem to."

I see the moment my words register.

Her eyebrows lift in horror. "Stay away? But why?"

Wasn't planning on unloading my heart tonight, but screw it.

"I can't just be your friend, Callie."

"Then don't," she says.

Ah, more of that young innocence. To cast all logic and reason aside for love. I want to. Oh, how badly I want to. The fairy in me demands I do so.

"You don't know what you're asking," I say, my eyes roving over her.

"I don't care."

I don't want to care either, but I'm neither an unseasoned youth, nor am I ruled by all the wild impulses my kind are known to have.

"But I do," I say with finality.

A tear leaks out of her eye.

I can't bear it. "Don't cry."

Couldn't even give her an evening without ruining it.

"You don't have to go," she pleads. "Everything can go back to the way it was. We can just...*pretend* tonight never happened."

Something in me breaks at her words. I feel about an inch tall.

I lean forward and kiss away her tears, knowing that I'm giving her mixed messages. "Just…give me some time," I say. I force myself to back away.

"How long are you going to be gone?" she asks.

As long as I can stand.

"Long enough to figure out what I want and what you deserve."

She must sense that tonight is different, that I crossed one of my own hard-fought lines. I can see her rising desperation.

"What about my debts?" she says.

"They don't matter." Not right now at least. So long as she owes me favors, the two of us are inextricably connected. I'm not worried about her slipping through my grasp. No, right now I'm still worried that the demon in me will decide taking her to the Otherworld is a great idea again.

I grab Callie's doorknob, trying to beat a hasty exit out of there.

"One final wish."

I hesitate. *Don't rise to the bait. Don't take the wish.* Already my magic is surging, ready to make yet another deal with my mate.

So hard to resist.

"Don't, Callie." I'm not sure I'll be able to say no.

She closes her eyes, her breath sighing out of her. "From flame to ashes, dawn to dusk, for the rest of our lives, be mine always, Desmond Flynn."

For a moment, I feel unbearable elation. My soul mate. This whole time I've been trying to avoid claiming her, and she ends the night by claiming *me*. How delightfully surprising.

In response to her words, my magic snaps out, lashing through the room. It absorbs her wish; I feel it—her desire, her intent, it's now mine.

And I know what this means—

A deal's been struck.

Desmond, you fucking fool. Should've left when you still had the chance.

She opens her eyes. For an instant she looks so hopeful it hurts.

I don't have time to tell her that it worked; that my magic accepted her deal. That until the end of time, the two of us are bound—not just by fate, not just by the beads on her wrist, but by the oath she recited.

I'm jerked away from her, thrust into the darkness and shot out miles away.

I hit the ground hard, the air knocked out of me. Slowly, I sit up, glancing around at the endless rolling hills that surround me on all sides.

My magic *betrayed* me. I didn't accept her deal; I didn't even think of her final words as one. But my power had. It set the terms of the bargain and bound us both to it.

It's been a long time since something like that's happened. I've known my power to be sentient, but normally *I* control *it* and not the other way around.

I suppose my control—or rather, my lack of it—is why this happened. And not only did it accept Callie's wish before I could even process it, it set the terms of her repayment.

My stomach plummets.

I'm afraid I already know what it took.

CHAPTER 20
REPAYMENT BEGINS

May, 7 years ago

My heart's been hammering in my chest since late last night.

For the thousandth time I try to materialize into Callie's dorm room. And for the thousandth time, I hit a magical wall that slingshots me back into the flat I've been renting in Dublin.

Gods, what has my magic done?

I try a different approach, appearing at the outskirts of the city of Peel. I move like a shadow through the city, heading closer and closer to the boarding school that houses my mate.

Peel Academy, Callie's school, rests on the very edge of the town, surrounded on three sides by sheer cliff faces and thrashing seas. It's tethered to the rest of Peel by a single, winding road.

I glimpse it in the distance, the coastal fog rolling between the buildings. Closer and closer I stalk, and for a few paltry minutes, my hope soars.

Whatever my magic took away, perhaps I can outmaneuver it.

I start up that narrow, winding road, heading for the campus grounds. I make it about five hundred feet outside of Peel Academy when my own, traitorous magic halts me. My feet won't move forward any farther. When I try to fly, my magic bars the airspace around the campus. When I melt into the night, becoming one with it, the darkness still won't let me come any closer.

I manifest back on the ground, and furiously I bash my fists against the invisible barrier, over and over again until my skin feels like it's been rubbed away and my bones have cracked themselves open. I might as well be hitting myself. This is my own magic that I'm coming up against.

Angry and defeated, I reluctantly return to my flat.

I run my hands through my hair.

Fuck, fuck, *fuck*.

I'm only now truly beginning to accept what I realized in that instant my power rose to meet Callie's final words: my magic granted my mate a favor, and now we're both paying its tithe.

I close my eyes and hear those last words all over again.

From flame to ashes, dawn to dusk, for the rest of our lives, be mine always, Desmond Flynn. Her voice is like a ghost in the room.

I try to hold onto her words. They're all I have left of her.

I suck in a breath. *They're all I have left.*

Suddenly, I'm desperate to touch every ridiculous souvenir she insisted she buy for me. I'm desperate to see her face in each one of my sketches. I begin to move through the flat, collecting the items I have of her from where they lay. A shot glass from Vegas, silks from Beirut, a beckoning cat from Tashirojima, a lamp from Marrakech, a beret from Paris— the list goes on and on.

I spread them around me, each one a talisman that can somehow protect me from the terrible truth: my magic fucked us both over.

Will Callie still love me once this magical tithe has been paid? Will she eventually piece together what has happened?

I need her to piece it together. Otherwise…

The uncertain future looms large.

You idiot, Desmond. Had you given a little more of yourself a little earlier, had you explained to her what your true feelings were, this might not have happened.

But what was I supposed to tell her? That she was fated to be my mate? That she really had no choice in the matter because she was mine?

I wasn't going to put that sort of pressure and those sorts of expectations on a teenage girl. Especially not one who'd only just escaped her stepfather's abuse.

I sit heavily on my bed.

What was my magic thinking? I gave her all those beads so that I could remain close to her for years to come. Not so I'd be forced to keep my distance.

If only I understood the precise terms of this repayment. But just as the lungs can breathe and the heart can beat even when you're unaware of them, so too can my magic act without my conscious consent.

It usually doesn't—like the heart and lungs it only works involuntarily when it needs to. And for whatever reason, it felt this deal was one it needed to make.

I just thought I'd have more time.

CHAPTER 21
ANOTHER MAN

3 years ago

Every day I try.

And every day I fail.

I toss the shots of Patrón back, one after the next, the alcohol burning my throat as it goes down. I don't bother with limes or salt. I want to feel the bite of the tequila, the burn of the pain.

The photo sits heavy in my pocket. I can't bear to look at it again; I can't bear to get rid of it either.

I've savored almost all the information I've learned of Callie since we've been apart. How much of a ballbuster she is now, how resourceful she can be. How she could've used her voice to become a singer or her body to become a model, but instead, she used her wits and her spirit to become a private investigator.

I've savored almost all the information I've learned… except for this.

That face I dream about, with those smiling eyes and beguiling mouth. Right now they're looking at another man, kissing another mouth, and I have the proof of it in my pocket.

A hot wave of jealousy rises up in me.

Damnit, I can't get the photo out of my mind, though it's been over an hour since I last looked at it. The tight embrace the two shared outside the man's apartment. I can taste bile at the back of my throat.

Should've been me.

I didn't want to know the rest of what happened between the two, but I learned it nonetheless. How she joined him inside the apartment, how she didn't leave until the early hours of the morning, slipping away like a villain from the scene of a crime, her clothes a little disheveled, her hair a little messy.

I flag down the waiter for another shot. When he slides it to me and I throw it back, the tequila tastes like water.

How long I've waited for my mate, and how quickly she was snatched just beyond my reach.

I have a rare moment of self-pity.

I'm the powerless bastard all those fae thought I was growing up. And the human mate my father derided me for, the one I spent decades denying, is now being pleasured by some other man while I sit here, numbing my sorrows on mortal brew.

Just as quickly as the pity comes, it burns away. Taking its place is anger—dark, smoldering anger.

I need to pound my fist into flesh.

I throw a few twenties on the table and leave the bar, going through my list of clients and homing in on the meanest motherfuckers who were never planning on paying me back without a fight. When I lay into them tonight, I'll imagine it's a different face, a different man.

Anything to dull this ache and expel this anger.

Perhaps I'll even leave my business card behind as a tantalizing breadcrumb that the Politia can add to their ever-thickening file on me. Maybe it'll even catch Callie's notice. You never know.

Regardless, it's about time I reminded humans why the Bargainer is someone to fear.

PART III

TILL DARKNESS DIES

CHAPTER 22
REUNION

Less than a year ago

I pass through my Catalina home and out onto my back porch. The sun sets on the Pacific Ocean, lighting the sky on fire as it descends beneath the horizon.

Across the vast miles of sea that spreads out from beyond my property, I can just barely make out the hazy Malibu hills.

My chest aches at the sight.

She's somewhere over there, so close it feels like I could reach out and touch her, but so far, I despair I'll never feel her skin beneath my fingers again.

I force my wings to manifest, then spread them wide. They soak in the last dying rays of the sun.

I bend my knees, then with one great thrust, I leap into the sky.

Just as I do every other evening, I fly toward that distant California shore, aiming for Callie's house. It's become something of a ritual, trying to see just how close I can get to her before my magic stops me.

It's been seven years. Callie's no longer a teenager. She can now legally drink, gamble, buy cigarettes. I've missed an entire era of her life, and the loss burns deep. How much more will I have to miss? Will she be stooped and frail by the time I can wrap my arms around her again? I can feel the sands of her life slipping down the hourglass, bringing her closer and closer to death. It makes me fevered, panicked.

I fly on, watching the clouds turn from pale orange to cotton candy pink, to dusty lilac. Eventually, they blend in with the deep blue evening sky.

I steel myself as I near that elusive boundary that marks the edge of my reach. Malibu is near enough that I can differentiate the buildings dotting the land. Near enough to make me see clearly what I'm being denied.

I press on, waiting for the moment my power will force me to stop. I feel it several seconds before I reach the magical boundary. Like always, I push against it, battling my own power.

Only this time, something's different.

It's weaker, putting up less resistance as I slam a fist into it. It shudders, my disturbance like a ripple along a lake.

That's never happened.

Encouraged, I hit it with another blow. It doesn't give.

C'mon.

Gathering my power into my fist I strike it again, hard. This time, it's like a bomb detonating.

The magic explodes, hitting me square in the chest and throwing me backward. As I careen through the sky, I feel Callie's seven-year-old debt finally—*finally*—dissipate.

Paid in full.

I don't breathe as I right myself.

I rub my chest, feeling the last remnants of my magic slide back into me.

Gods' hands, it's *over*.

The wait is over.

I fly the rest of the way to Callie's beach house, my heart pounding furiously.

At last, I will be able to see her, feel her, breathe her in. There will be no more other men, no more long, lonely nights.

I land soundlessly on her property, my wings folding behind me. I can feel something in the air and in my bones, a magic drawn up from the core of the earth.

A thousand times I imagined returning to her as I am now, and every second of the flight that brought me here I agonized that somehow this wasn't real. Surely after all that waiting, it's not just over.

I run my fingers over an aged terracotta pot that sits on her patio, the succulent it holds spilling out from it. Her house, her things—I can touch them. The magic never let me before. I had to sustain myself on scraps of information up until now. For a man like me, the secrecy nearly killed me.

I'm seeing Callie's place for the first time. The inside is dark, and I can sense that at the moment, the place is empty. It stirs my blood into a frenzy, knowing that I'll have to wait even longer to see her again. Now that the debt's been paid, I have no patience for waiting.

I could always seek her out, but that sort of eagerness puts one at a disadvantage, and when it comes to reclaiming my mate, I have enough working against me as is—namely the fact that she must blame me for leaving her seven years ago.

Her sliding glass door snicks as the lock unlatches. Silently it slips open, and I step inside.

Callie's scent hits me, and it nearly brings me to my knees. How had I lasted this long without it?

My boots scuff against the gritty floor. I toe the sand that lays scattered along the ground, the unmistakable shape of half a footprint still visible.

Callie. My siren. Can't keep herself away from the ocean.

My footfalls sound heavy as I make my way through her living room. I pick up an empty wine bottle and read the label. Hermitage. I nearly whistle. Expensive taste.

I've heard enough about Callie to know it's not just wine she drinks. Whiskey is her other poison of choice, and if my information is correct—which it nearly always is—she enjoys her spirits more often than she should. The thought makes my gut twist uncomfortably. I introduced her to this particular vice, after all.

I set the bottle back down and move to the kitchen, my fingers trailing her cracked tile countertops. My gaze roves over the faded cabinets and the worn wood floors. She spent a pretty penny buying her seaside Malibu house, and yet by the looks of it, she hasn't changed a damn thing about it.

I move over to a hanging corkboard near her fridge, several notes pinned to it, mostly just phone numbers and a note with a smiley face drawn on it, signed *Temper* in the corner.

Leaving the kitchen, I head down her hallway. Her walls are bare of the usual photos that people mount. There're no family portraits—no surprise there—but there aren't any photos of Callie with friends.

Why?

I note with more than a touch of dismay that the trinkets

we collected from around the world, the ones that once filled her dorm room, are also absent.

The question now is: Are they missing because she's angry at me, or because she feels indifferent?

Please not indifference. I can work with anything but that.

The only things that hang on the walls are some framed watercolors of coral and a carved wooden fish; the generic sort of shit that you can buy at any store.

I pass her guest bathroom, then another room that looks like it's sometimes a guest room, sometimes a storage space. Casting a bit of my magic out, I listen to the shadows, letting them gossip to me about this house and its owner.

...drinks in the dark hours...

...shower busted down the hall...

...talks in her sleep about lost love...

...several men have stayed the night...

Hot jealousy roars within me at that last one. Here I stand, the man once famous for bedding much of the Otherworld's female population, now torn in two when suddenly the tables are turned on me.

No men save me will warm her bed any longer.

Speaking of—Callie's bedroom looms ahead. Just the sight of the door has my wings flaring. I head inside, my eyes drinking in the space. Everywhere I look there's a testament to the sea—from more marine wall art to a conch shell sitting on a side table to vases filled with sea glass. Because she can't live in the sea...she brought it to her. It even has the briny smell of salt and seaweed.

I move through the room, skimming my fingers over the spines of novels shoved into a whitewashed bookshelf.

It's only when I get to one of the side chairs in her room

that I come across something that doesn't belong. I pick up the offensive piece of clothing, which was thrown over the chairback, and bring it to my nose.

I breathe in the material, then grimace, squeezing the cloth tight in my fist.

Dog. Specifically, a lycanthrope.

A bit of my inner darkness taints my eagerness.

Her…lover.

For a brief moment, I'd forgotten.

From what I've gathered, she's been dating a Politia bounty hunter. At first, I didn't believe it. Callypso Lillis, the woman who once quaked at the authorities, now dates one of them?

I shouldn't have been so surprised. Sirens are a bit fatalistic. They have a long history of getting themselves into trouble thanks to a millennia-old curse placed upon their species. And even though that curse has since been lifted, there will always be a part of my mate's kind that will attract trouble.

Though technically, between me and the bounty hunter, I'm the worse choice.

It only takes a little magic for flames to begin licking the material. Within seconds, the offending shirt is nothing more than smoke and ashes, and then it's not even that, my magic eating up every last trace of its existence.

I hope Eli enjoyed Callie while he had her. Now that she and I have paid our tithe, I have no plans to let her go again.

By the time Callie arrives at her house, I've thoroughly made myself at home. I raided her kitchen, smirking when I came across a secret stash of sweets—because who the hell is she

198

hiding her sweets from?—and frowning when I came across her secret stash of half-drunk spirits. Those I know she must hide from herself, only taking them out when she's too weak or beaten down to resist.

After throwing together a meal for myself, I flipped through her Netflix account. By all appearances she still likes book-to-movie adaptations, and she also watches a good dose of comedy shows.

Now I recline on her bed, gazing at the moon, which rises over the Pacific. The sight stirs some old yearning in me, something both nostalgic and dully painful. Maybe it's the sight of that moon so close to the water—so close and yet still out of reach. It reminds me of Nyxos and Fierion, the gods of night and day; the star-crossed lovers always seeking each other, always kept apart.

But the thrill of being back in her life is too heady for me to get sad at the rising moon. I bathe in the shadows that slip through Callie's windows, closing my eyes while I wait.

Eventually, I hear the front door creak open, then the soft sound of footfalls. It takes my mate entirely too long to make her way back to her bedroom, where I lounge on her mattress.

It's taking all my concentration to keep my wings and my eagerness in check.

Callie steps into the doorway, her body cast in shadows.

By the gods.

Can't be real.

Not that dark hair that falls in waves down her body, not that face, which was created to break men's hearts and bend their wills. My gaze moves to her flesh, encased in only the wispiest lingerie.

She's a vision made to haunt me.

Before I can help it, my wings manifest beneath me, flaring open. I'm the teenager and she's the unattainable woman.

How ironic the Fates are.

My wings are out only for the briefest of moments, but the movement startles her. I hear her swift intake of air, and then a moment later, she flicks on the bedroom lights.

Fuck me good, nothing has ever looked so godsdamned appealing as Callie in lingerie. She looked mesmerizing in the shadows; she's a vision in the soft light of her room.

All signs of the girl she once was are now gone. Teenage Callie has been replaced by this creature, with her womanly curves and a devastating face.

Time to scheme, Desmond. It's going to take more than sheer ardor to conquer my mate's heart.

Callie stares at me, shocked. No, not shocked—*thunderstruck.* I catch a peek of unsure teenage Callie in the look.

There's my girl.

I flick my gaze over her. "You've upgraded your lingerie since I last saw you."

Going to dream about this later.

There's a long pause; Callie appears to be collecting herself.

"Hello, Desmond Flynn," she finally says, deliberately using my full name. She might as well have reached between my legs and squeezed my balls.

A slow grin parts my lips. Feisty thing. "I didn't realize you wanted to spill secrets tonight, Callypso Lillis."

My eyes return to her flesh. I can't keep myself from looking at her, *all* of her.

Take. Claim. Keep.

She cuts across her bedroom, grabbing a robe from her closet.

"What do you want, Des?" she asks from where she ties the robe. Her voice is somehow annoyed, bored, and exasperated all at once. There's a name for this.

Apathy.

For one split second the sky feels like it's crashing down around me.

She's moved on entirely.

But then I notice how her hands tremble.

Relief washes through me.

She's shaken by this too. My luck hasn't entirely run out then.

Like a predator, I pounce on her vulnerability.

I materialize behind her in an instant, bending to her ear. "Demanding as always, I see." I smile a little when she yelps in surprise, turning to face me. "Odd character flaw of yours, considering how much *you* owe *me.*"

My magic slips into my voice, promising her all those forbidden things that her insatiable siren craves.

I will give each and every one of them to you, siren, night after night, so long as you're mine.

Those deep, fathomless eyes of hers search my face. I forgot what it felt like to be seen by them. Seven years has made them sadder, lonelier, but no less piercing.

She does believe I abandoned her. Clear as starlight, I read it on her face.

In that instant, I come as close as I ever have to freely giving up information. Only centuries of restraint hold my tongue. Telling Callie the truth doesn't buy me love. She's had years to resent me; a few short sentences aren't going to just fix that.

I'm going to have to make her fall in love with me, all over again.

I take her hand and push up the sleeve of her robe. Row after row of my beads twist up her forearm. A primal sort of pleasure stirs in me at the sight.

"My bracelet still looks good on you, cherub."

I can ask anything of her, anything at all, and she must oblige me. I could ask her to live with me, to marry me, to bed me, to bear my children.

It's not enough. Not nearly. I want her love, her thoughts, her passion—and I want it to be given freely. Always freely. Nothing less will do.

But she doesn't know this.

"Callie, you owe me a lot of favors."

You're mine. You don't know it yet, love, but you are.

She meets my gaze, and I feel the weight of her dawning realization. A part of her understands this is the end—and it's the beginning. "You're finally here to collect."

CHAPTER 23
TILL DARKNESS DIES

Less than a year ago

This isn't the first time I've brought Callie to my realm, but it feels like it.

My heart races as I hold my mate in my arms, the stars around us glittering like gems as I fly toward Somnia. I can't stop looking at her—which isn't some new revelation—her face has always drawn me in. But now, as I carry her across the Otherworld and to my palace, my head is filled with thoughts of truly making her mine.

All because she stroked my cock to release this morning.

On the outside, I'm still the same slick sonuvabitch I always am. Inside, I'm squealing like a kid getting cake. Now that the door to intimacy has officially been opened, there isn't an ounce of reserve left inside of me. I'm already making plans—about watching Callie come apart on my fingers, my tongue, my cock—I want it all—on keeping her in my house and in my bed. On marrying her and making her my queen. On having lots and lots of babies with her.

Basically, I'm dreaming up all sorts of fun, freaky shit that would probably scare her off if I uttered a word of it now.

It's really fucking convenient that I know how to keep a secret when I want to.

As soon as Somnia comes into view, I make a beeline for the palace. Last time we were here there was all sorts of fanfare. This time our entrance will be much more private.

I land on one of the castle's back terraces, my wings folding at my back as I set Callie on her feet.

"No fancy entrance this time?" she says.

"Tonight I didn't want to share you," I say, using my magic to mask my wings and call forth my war bands and crown.

Callie flashes me a smile, one that reaches her eyes. If I were walking, I would've stumbled. I don't deserve those looks of hers, but I will happily take each and every one of them.

I set take her hand, leading her into my palace.

Various fae bustle about inside. They bow and murmur greetings and act as though everything is normal, despite the fact that most of them can't stop staring at Callie. I don't blame them—my mate is a vision. Who needs the moon when she is here to draw us in like the tide?

I lead her through the halls of the palace, out across the grounds, and then into the building that houses my rooms.

My normally steady heart hammers away as I step up to the door of my rooms. My quarters have been cold and lonely for as long as I can remember, and I've never brought a woman here—not like this.

I open the door and usher Callie in, entering behind her. My shadows curl around me I watch her take it all in.

Seeing her in my space…it's doing weird things to my heart. I want her to love it. My basest fae urges rise up.

She is your mate. Take—claim—keep.

I want to see all that dark hair of hers spread like spilled ink against my sheets. I want her wet and wanton and coming apart in my bed. I want my room to smell like her so that even after I somehow manage to let her leave, a part of her will remain here.

I can barely breathe through my own want.

I catch Callie's hand and brush my lips against her knuckles.

"Truth or dare?" I whisper.

Her eyes sparkle like gems as she focuses her attention on me. She looks a little breathless, and she must know exactly where my mind is at.

Gods, please pick—

"Dare."

Yes.

Feeling victorious, I drag my siren into my arms, giving into the desire that's ridden me hard since this morning.

Take—

My mouth finds Callie's, and I press a searing kiss to those soft lips.

Claim—

My lips don't leave her, even after the kiss could've rightfully ended. I want to drown in the taste of her—I *will* drown in the taste of her.

Keep—

I scoop her into my arms and carry her through my chambers and into my bedroom, kissing her all the while.

I can sense her curiosity—Callie still wants to take in every last detail of these chambers. I find that once I lay her out on my bed, I want to take everything in as well. My space looks so much better with her in it. It's no longer my cold chambers that I stay in only long enough to rest. Now that she's here, I want to linger.

You have taken her to your world, now claim her so thoroughly she will never want to leave it.

I drop to my knees, my hand caressing Callie's leg. Gods, but I need to fight my own eagerness so that I can draw this out.

Callie leans forward, brushing back some of my white-blond hair so that she can see my face. I lean into her intoxicating touch.

Claim!

I move my free hand to her other leg, hoping she doesn't notice just how much they tremble. This woman undoes me like nothing else can.

"Once the repayment begins, the magic takes on a life of its own, Callie," I warn her. Already I can feel my power gathering. "Do you still want my dare?"

Callie hesitates. She has felt the brush of my magic; she understands that once we begin our little dare, we will have to see it through to the end.

And with me kneeling between her legs, my hands on her flesh, what I'm really asking is, *Are you sure about being intimate with me?*

"Yes," she says softly.

I want to shout in triumph. Even after all the pain our separation has caused her, she still wants this with me. My resilient siren.

Going to make you come so hard, I silently promise her. I want my magic and my mouth to become her new vices.

My magic unspools, thickening in the air around us. I know she must already be feeling it.

I drag my sweet siren to the edge of the bed, reveling in the way her dress gathers around her waist I smooth my hands over her legs, letting them travel up to her lacy panties.

"How I have imagined..." I murmur, relishing the moment, "and it has never done you justice."

My heart is hammering and my breath is catching in disbelief that I can finally touch my siren the way I have longed to.

I was made to give this woman pleasure.

Slowly, I peel Callie's panties away. I get my first good look at Callie's pussy, and I have to bite back my groan. She's already wet, and fuck is this the most erotic view. My cock is hard as a rock.

"Cherub," I say, tossing her panties aside. Can't take my eyes off her pussy. "I am going to make you feel good. So, so good."

I push her dress up further and begin to press soft kisses on that stretch of skin low on her pelvis.

Gods, so fucking erotic.

"Des..."

She sounds as tightly wound as I feel.

I run a finger down the slit of her sex, forcing myself to go slow and to keep my touch light.

Callie gasps, and oh, I like that. So I tease her slit again. This time her hips buck, and I can't seem to stop the low, hungry sound that slips from my lips.

I slip a finger into her core, and I have to bite back a moan at the warm grip her pussy has on that digit. She's *so* wet.

Going to taste incredible.

I add another finger, feeling her walls stretch at the intrusion, and I'm rewarded with a low moan from Callie.

"That's it, Callie," I say, stroking her. I can feel the edge of my own fae hunger creeping forth.

Need to taste her.

"Des." She says my name like a desperate plea.

I remove my fingers from her core and lick them one by one.

Gods.

I groan at the taste. "Better than my imagination."

And I want more. So much more.

I grab one of Callie's legs and hitch it over my shoulder. The other I widen, just so that I can see her pussy all the better. I want this to be filthy. I want to feast on my cherub's juices and coat myself in them.

That hunger roars in me, and it's all I can do to lift my gaze to Callie's.

"Fair warning: I'm not stopping until you come."

I press my lips to her, biting back another groan at her taste. I don't know if it's a siren thing or a soul mate thing, but she tastes like heaven.

I lick all around her core, my teeth grazing over her sensitive flesh. Almost immediately her hips buck against me, and the most intoxicating sounds fall from her lips.

Her reaction is almost as delicious as her pussy itself.

"My cherub. So sweet, so responsive," I murmur, my own desire threading through my voice.

We are just getting started.

For a while I continue on just as I am, licking and grazing and nipping.

My cock is so swollen it's ready to rip through the seam of my trousers.

Here's to hoping I don't come in my pants twice in one day.

Then again, for this moment it might be worth it.

Callie is making the breathiest noises and her hips are moving against my face, and it's all so delectable and civilized. I think my siren believes this is how I plan on eating her out to completion.

I smile briefly against her skin.

My sweet, naive siren. That is not how the King of the Night does oral.

I move my attention to her clit, and then my mouth proceeds to have a very long and lurid love affair with it.

Callie's skin brightens, her hips are bucking helplessly against me, and I don't think I've ever been as turned on in my life as I am in this moment.

Then she tries to cut and run from my mouth.

"Ah, ah, cherub," I say, dragging her hips back into the cradle of my arms, "you're not going anywhere. Not until I'm finished with you."

She's panting and out of sorts and gods, I'm not nearly finished tasting her.

I move my mouth back to her clit, licking and sucking and mouthing silent odes to that most sensitive section of flesh. It's messy and my face is covered in her fluids, and the luridness of it all is only making my cock throb harder.

Callie lets out a strangled sob. "Des, *please*."

I want to drag this on for longer. I want to spend the entire day right here, edging my mate to near insanity just so that she can come harder than she ever has.

We have an endless future for bed play, I have to remind myself. *I can start off...tame.*

So I settle for sucking on her clit and watching her lose herself to sensation.

"Come for me," I breathe against her flesh.

"*Des,*" Callie says, lost in sensation. She's thrashing in my sheets, sullying them up exactly how I hoped she might.

"Come," I demand.

"*Oh my god, Des.*" The siren is threaded through her voice, and there is nothing sexier than hearing the ethereal sound of my name on my mate's lips as she orgasms, her skin glowing brightly.

I suck her clit as she rides it out, lingering there until I sense her climax retreating. Only then do I move my lips away, exchanging my open-mouthed kisses for soft, chaste ones that I rain down her inner thighs.

Callie's legs slip from my shoulders. I catch and close them, pulling her dress back down. Gathering my siren to me, I move us to the head of my bed. For a moment, I bask in the feel of my soul mate in my arms and my sheets, her taste on my lips.

That alone fills me with the sort of joy I've been chasing like an addict for these last several years.

Callie turns those dark eyes on me, and gods, but she's looks at me as though I might've actually invented oral. My ego shoots through the roof.

"That was…" She searches for the words.

I think of the years I longed for her. Of the fantasies I vowed I'd shower her with as soon as I got my hands on her.

"A long time in coming," I finish.

Cannot believe she's mine. The thought overwhelms me, and I lean in and kiss her. The second her skin brightens I remember that she must be able to taste herself on me.

I can't wait to explore every last desire Callie has.

I trail my fingers across her arm.

"What are you thinking about?" she asks, watching me far too closely.

"So much, cherub." It's an easier response than letting her know that I'm already plotting our future.

"I've imagined you in my bed a thousand times," I continue as Callie fingers my war bands.

"A thousand times?" I see hope burning in her eyes, and it nearly does me in.

She wants this as much as I do.

"Do you want to know a truth of mine?" I breathe against her ear.

"Always," she says, greedy for more of my secrets.

I will give them all to you, so long as you promise to be mine.

I take Callie's hand and press it to my heart, letting her discover one of my most vulnerable secrets.

Her eyes widen as she feels how it races. Slowly, her eyes rise to meet mine.

I can see her disbelief, and it gives me the courage to admit this truth of mine to her.

"It does that whenever I'm around you."

———

Back on earth, the bounty hunter is a threat no more. That much is obvious the moment he sets foot on my Catalina property and sees my wings. He recognizes what they mean.

It all goes over Callie's head. But she must have some sort of idea. After my confrontation with Eli, she locks herself away in her room, her face troubled.

My body practically quakes with the need to be close to her. Just like the night of the dance, I'm losing my control. My fae instincts are crowding out reason.

Eventually the door to Callie's room opens and she storms out. "Is it true?" she demands.

I glance at her, still distracted by my thoughts. "Is what true?"

"About your *wings*," she says. "Is it true that you've been flashing them to let everyone know that I belong to you? That I'm your betrothed?"

I still. She's come awfully close to the truth—she missed the mark, but gods, she's close.

My heart is picking up.

My mate. *Claim her.*

My magic is spilling out of me, darkening the room. All those years of denying myself; I'm about to crack us wide open.

"It *is*," she says, shocked.

I approach Callie, who looks spitting mad.

Claim her.

"You *bastard*," she swears. "Were you ever going to tell me?"

If I admit to her the truth, I won't let her slip away again.

Is she ready for that?

The devil knows I am.

She pokes me in the chest. "Were. You?"

I glance down at her finger, my good nature slipping away as she challenges me. My darker impulses rise to the surface.

I let a smile slip out as I step in closer to her, our chests touching. "Are you sure you want to know my secrets, cherub?" I say. "They will cost you much more than a wrist full of beads."

"Des, I just want answers from you."

Take—claim—keep.

I pick up a lock of her hair. "What can I say? Fairies can be incredibly jealous, selfish lovers."

Understatement.

"You should've told me."

Told her when precisely? In high school, when she was too young? Or when I finally managed to return to her side after seven years apart? Because that would've been a great icebreaker.

"Perhaps I was proud to have my wings out," I say. "Perhaps I enjoyed the way you looked at them and the way others looked at them. Perhaps I felt things that I haven't felt before."

I let my wings unfurl, careful to release them slowly. My magic is all-consuming. If I were to completely give into it now, it would cloak the room into darkness and release all sorts of pheromones that a siren would be especially suscep-tible to. I want Callie to come to me of her own volition.

"Perhaps," I continue, "I didn't want to tell you only to find out that you didn't feel the same. I know how to be lethal, Callie. I know how to be just. I don't know how to deal with you. With us. With this."

For so long I've been the ruthless Bargainer and the fierce King of Night; I haven't had practice being simply a man in love. I'm afraid I'm going to blow it.

"With what?"

She's going to make me spell it out. I can feel my heart banging against my rib cage. When it comes to Callie, I want to give her my secrets, but her reaction also has the power to undo me.

I trace her collarbone. "I haven't been wholly honest with you," I say carefully.

Not exactly a shocking revelation.

"There was a question that you asked me," I continue. "*Why now?* I've been gone seven years, Callie. So why do I come back now?"

Her brows knit. "You needed my help," she says.

I *had* asked for her help solving the disappearances of hundreds of fairies in my kingdom. But surely she can see that for the smoke screen it is.

"A lie that became the truth," I say.

Put the pieces together, Callie. They're right there in front of you.

But of course, she won't. She can't. I've kissed her on the lips and between her thighs—I all but moved her into my home—yet she sees none of it for what it is. Because even after seven years, she still is that lonely girl that doesn't believe she's allowed to love and be loved.

I gently touch her cheek. "*Callie.*"

Can't she tell that she brings me to my knees? Morning, evening, and night, she's always right there in every beat of my heart. That sweet voice of hers sings through my veins. It calls to me across worlds. Everything she is, is mine, and everything I am is hers. Always.

I spread my wings fully out, the tips of them nearly brushing the walls of my living room.

Gods it feels good to finally expose them. Fought this for too long.

"A fairy doesn't show his wings to his betrothed."

I move my hand to the back of her neck, stroking the skin there softly. It still fills me with wonder that I get to be near her. That once again I can finally touch her. She's not the only one who thought that this was too good to be true.

"A fairy shows them to his soul mate."

She stills.

Seven years of pain, seven years of waking up with the same damn ache that never goes away. Maybe tonight I can finally put that anguish to bed, once and for all.

"You lie," she breathes, disbelief coating her voice.

I know the feeling. Like she can't bear to believe it because it might break her. No, it *will* break her. It will break her, and she'll never be the same. It's already broken me.

"No, cherub, I'm not."

She searches my face. "So you're saying…"

"That I'm in love with you? That I have been since you were that obstinate teen with way too much courage? That you're my soul mate and I'm yours? Gods save me, yes I am."

Callie reels a little back, her eyes widening and her lips parting. One of her hands touches her chest, right over her heart.

She must feel the rightness of it. The same way the river flows downstream, the same way night follows day and the sun rises in the east and sets in the west. We were always meant to be.

She searches my face. "But you left."

"I did," I agree. "But I never meant to stay away."

"Then why did you?"

Her eyes have that same haunted look they had back when I first met her, only now it's my transgressions and not her stepfather's that are responsible for it.

I run a hand through my hair, feeling like the world's worst soul mate. "You were so damn young," I explain. *Never meant to hurt you.* "And you'd been abused. And my heart chose you. I felt it that first night, but I didn't believe it, not until the feeling grew until it couldn't be ignored."

How to explain our bond? It defies the logic of both our worlds and our magic.

It's like someone bottled up her essence, and I drank it all in. It simmers beneath my skin. It's recognition so primal, so pure, there are no words to describe it. It defies the senses—it defies even magic.

"I couldn't stay away," I continue, "I could barely resist you at all, but I didn't want to push you into something. Not when you'd just escaped a man that took and took. I didn't want you to think that was all men were good for."

She stares at me, a tear escaping her eyes. Another follows.

I feel my secrets unburdening themselves. A part of me expected that. What I hadn't expected was for them to unburden *her*.

I brush Callie's tears away. *Should've done this much sooner.*

"So I let you play your game, buying favor after favor from me," I say, "until the day I couldn't take it. No mate of mine should *owe* me."

When had it started to feel wrong? I can't remember the date, only the sensation—like a brand pressed under my own skin, shame burning me from the inside out.

"But my magic," I explain, "it has a mind of its own... like your siren, I can't always control it. It thought that the more you owed me, the longer I could guarantee that you were in my life. Of course, that strategy came to an abrupt end the moment you cast your final wish."

That's when all my crafty plans came crashing down. I was sabotaged by my own power.

"That final wish of yours," I continue, "it was bigger than either of us. You wanted me, I was falling for you, and it wasn't right, Callie. I knew it wasn't right. Not when you were sixteen. But I could be patient. For my little siren, my mate, I could."

I already waited centuries for her. Had she needed it, I could wait centuries more. In theory. That's what I told myself every time I got too close and had to flee. That keeping my distance was in her best interest, that I was strong enough to endure this sweet agony.

Fucking lies, all of it.

I wasn't strong enough. After the night of Callie's dance, had I managed to leave before her last wish, I might've kept my distance for a week, maybe two. I doubt I could've lasted a month.

My magic, as it turns out, is far, far stronger than my will ever was.

"But that wish..." I say, remembering that fateful evening. "I was a prisoner to it."

"What *wish*?" she asks, looking lost.

The one that kept me from you. All this time, and she still has no idea.

"Your last one," I say. "On the night of the dance— 'From flame to ashes, dawn to dusk, for the rest of our lives, be mine always, Desmond Flynn.'"

Those words have been seared into me. Callie might never know just how many lonely nights I murmured them to myself. Or that I've sketched the look on her face when she spoke them a hundred times, trying to capture and recapture everything she was and wanted in that moment. All so that I could hold onto her while we were apart.

Her face heats. "You never granted that one."

I tilt my head just the slightest. "Are you sure about that?"

The flush dies away from her skin. She looks like someone doused her in ice water.

"You...you granted it?" she says.

"I did."

What I'd give not to have. How our lives would've been different if that hadn't happened. I have to hope that my magic knew something I didn't; that this was the better road to take.

Callie's eyes move to her bracelet. "But the beads never showed up..."

"They wouldn't, since you were already paying them off. We both were." Damn my magic for that.

Slowly her gaze rises to meet mine. "What do you mean?" she breathes.

"A favor as large as the one you requested requires steep payment," I say. "Do you think my magic would allow you to buy yourself a mate so easily? That kind of favor requires a good dose of heartbreak and years of waiting—seven years, to be precise."

Seven years that are finally, thankfully, over.

"Every day after your last wish, I worked myself raw trying to get close to you." The sheer agony of it all. "And every day I was stopped by my very own magic, which had turned on me."

Callie begins to shake, and I can see all that brittle bitterness of hers falling away. Peering out from beneath it, she's that same innocent girl she's always been. Though perhaps *innocent* is the wrong word. Perhaps *hopeful* is a better one.

"Then one day," I say, "the magic's hold on me loosened. I tried to approach you like I had a thousand times before, and this time, the magic didn't stop me.

"Finally, after the longest seven years of my life, I was able to come back to my love, my mate. The sweet siren that loved my darkness, and my bargains, and my company when I was no one and nothing more than Desmond Flynn. The woman that took fate into her own hands when she spoke those ancient vows and declared herself mine."

It's dawning on her. This is real. *We* are real.

All those evenings she watched me leave her, those

are the illusion. Because the truth is, I have searched worlds for her, looked for her for centuries. I've held her a thousand times in my dreams, and I have died a thousand times upon waking.

My heart, my soul. My queen.

"Callie," I say, "I love you. I've loved you from the beginning. And I will love you long after the last star dies. I will love you until the end of darkness itself."

"You love me," she says, trying the words out.

"I love you, Callypso Lillis." *I love you. I love you. I love you.*

It's finally out there between us, that beautiful, brutal truth. And now all I want is to fall into her and never return. My sweet redemption.

For several seconds she takes me in, the only movement the rise and fall of her chest.

And then she smiles.

Ah, Gods! Who needs the sun when she smiles like that? She can make sadness forget it exists.

"Do you…want to be with me?" she asks.

She still doesn't get it.

I pull her into me, staring down at those wide, hopeful eyes. "Callie, this may be oversharing, but I'm getting the sense that you want that at the moment…"

Her smile widens. "I do."

So I tell her all those truths that should be so painfully obvious right now. Because I'm a sentimental fucker and she's my mate.

"I want to wake up every morning to you, cherub, and one day, in the future, when I've made myself worthy of it, I want to marry the shit out of you, and then I want to have lots and lots of babies with you. If, that is, you will have me."

I want that future so badly and I want her to want it too.

Please want it, Callie. Please want me.

She doesn't speak, and one agonizing second gives way to the next.

"I'll be yours, if you'll be mine," she finally says.

I feel my grin nearly split my face in two, and my wings flare wider than ever.

Take. Claim. Keep.

Nothing, *nothing*, feels as good as this moment.

This is what it's like to be loved. Like the universe forming from chaos. It's lighter than air and headier than magic. It's everything.

"I'll always be yours, cherub." Even when she doesn't want my crafty ass. I've never *not* been hers.

I cup her cheeks.

There's a vow, an ancient vow, in my land, and as long as anyone can remember, lovers have whispered it under the stars. For seven years they've eaten away at me. Finally I set them free.

I search her eyes. "And mountains may rise and fall, and the sun might wither away, and the sea claim the land and swallow the sky. But you will always be mine. And the stars might fall from the heavens, and night might cloak the earth, but until darkness dies, I will always be yours."

CHAPTER 24
THE KING OF CLAWS AND TALONS

Less than a year ago

When I wake up the next morning, Callie's vanished—only, sirens don't vanish. They glamour and beguile, but they don't altogether disappear, particularly ones who've been magically bound to live under my roof.

After last night, could she have fled me as I used to flee her? The mere thought is enough to level me.

She loves you, you fool. She wouldn't flee.

I move through my Catalina house, but there's no sign of her. I check the front door. It's locked from the inside. She has a key, but at the moment it's sitting on a side table off the entryway.

The back door then.

When I come to it, it's unlatched. I feel my relief sigh out of me.

She came out here to be close to the water, of course.

But when I walk outside, there's no sign of her. My unease

gathers. I stride deeper into my backyard, stopping at my patio table. A full cup of coffee rests on the table. I pick up the mug.

Cool to the touch.

It's just one of those things that scream something's off.

If Callie could, she'd mainline her caffeine in the morning. She wouldn't leave her coffee undrunk.

My unease becomes something else. It feels like someone is squeezing and twisting my gut.

I feed magic to the few shadows that linger out here. They will know what happened. A few seconds later, my power boomerangs back to me, the shadows remaining obstinately silent. Earth's shadows love to chat. The only time they've ever remained quiet is when…

Gods above and below.

There's only one being the shadows stay silent for. It's same being who's behind the fae disappearances. The same monster who has been sending the women back in glass coffins, their bodies trapped in an unnatural sleep, newborn babies clutched in their stiff embraces.

No. Impossible.

Callie's a mortal, and the Thief of Souls has very particular taste. He wouldn't come here, he wouldn't take her.

But if…if he did take her, then it's my fault. I'd tasked her with this case, never imagining that she'd catch the attention of the monster I hunted.

Should've known better, Desmond. Monsters always notice what you care about.

A second later, I dissipate into the shadows.

Need to find her. I chant the sentence over and over as I begin my search.

All day and all night, I scour worlds for her. Earth, the Otherworld, she could be in either.

The task would be infinitely easier if our bond was fully in place. But because it's not, because Callie is a human and I am a fairy, I can't reach through our shaky connection to locate her.

Instead, I search the old-fashioned way, cashing in favors for information. I beseech the shadows of both my world and hers, looking for any little tidbit of knowledge they'll give me. But the darkness is silent, and it makes me want to destroy something.

Though the shadows tell me nothing, if I focus hard and long enough, I swear they quake with fear. I've wondered a thousand times what would cause the night to feel fear. Now, I'm too consumed by my own panic to dwell on that question.

The Thief of Souls *has* Callie. The darkness may as well have said as much.

My mind flashes to all those female warriors trapped in their glass coffins, a baby clutched to their breasts. Before now I felt a spark of sorrow for them—sorrow and horror—but that was it. They were not my loved ones, my family or friends.

Now, I'm coming up with all sorts of terrible explanations for how those women came to be sleeping…and how they acquired a child.

Rage is burning through the fear. I will *break* the Otherworld in two before that happens to Callie.

———————

Several days in, all my cashed-in favors and whispering shadows get me nowhere.

I storm through my palace, making myself at home deep in the dungeons. I perch on a stool and steeple my fingers, tapping them against my mouth.

Forget about what you know of the Thief of Souls, Desmond, what unusual occurrences have happened to Callie? Monsters love leaving their calling cards. I should know.

There was the ripped-up mattress, the dream that was so obviously not *just* a dream. And then there were the visions that the casket children had shown her—visions of cages and an antlered creature.

That's all I have.

It's going to have to be enough.

I start with the antlered beast. There are many horned fae in the Otherworld, but only one with any distinction—

Karnon Kaliphus, Master of Animals, Lord of the Wild Heart, King of Fauna—and lately, the Mad King.

He just might have enough power and lunacy to fit the bill.

Shit, but am I really assuming the Fauna King is behind the disappearances?

Those who are moon-touched are capable of much. The question is, could Karnon be capable of the evil wrought by the Thief of Souls?

Surely one of his subjects would've said something. Surely, if he were truly guilty, *someone* would've noticed something damnable by now.

Cannot afford to ignore this possibility. It's the best lead I've got. For Callie's sake, I have to assume the worst of Karnon.

But if I'm wrong…not only will I be no closer to finding her, I might have a war on my hands. That's what happens when you attack kings.

War for Callie if you must, but find her!

As swift as the night, I leave the dungeons of Somnia and make my way to the Fauna Kingdom. Being the king of a rival kingdom, I'm required to announce my presence in my fellow ruler's territory. I don't bother.

If I'm right and Karnon's behind this, then his soldiers are behind it as well. No one keeps a secret this big all to themselves.

I join with the night sky, sweeping across the Kingdom of Fauna. I'm no longer a man, no longer a body with arms and legs and a face. I'm hardly a thing at all. More like sentient darkness.

The shadows are ever quiet here. I feel it then as I never have. Old magic. Powerful magic. The kind not written down in books. Perhaps it's not that the shadows won't share their secrets; perhaps it's that they can't.

If Karnon is the one wielding this kind of magic, then I've vastly underestimated him.

Before I head to Fauna's capitol, I scour what I can of the land, looking for any trace of Callie. I come up with nothing.

Just as I thought.

There's a chance that she's simply not here in the Kingdom of Fauna, but there's also a chance that she's in a protected area of the palace, where wards prevent me from entering.

All the kingdoms have pockets of space that are spelled against me and the other rulers. This way, rival kings and queens can't just waltz in and learn their most closely guarded secrets.

I linger outside of Karnon's castle, my essence spread across the darkness. Things are almost painfully normal. Guards make their circuits around the perimeter, Fauna nobility come and go. I follow several of them back to their homes, waiting for one of them to slip up, but none of them do.

You were wrong, Desmond. She's not here.

Callie could be in another kingdom—even another world—enduring cruelties I can't fathom.

I'm considering leaving my post when strange magic wafts through the darkness. It's so faint I almost miss it. With it comes the urge to coalesce back into my form. Reluctantly, I do so, my body manifesting in a tree downwind from the palace.

I feel the magic stir again, this time concentrating over my heart. I draw in a shocked breath, my hand pressing against my chest.

Gods above, I *feel* her.

My mate.

Callie's essence is a song, something I imagined sirens might sing to wayward men. Only it resonates inside me, calling me to her.

A second later I realize I *shouldn't* sense her. Our magic is too incompatible. The weak bond between us thrums, and through it I sense *distress.* Immense distress. It's so intense it managed to bridge the chink in our connection.

The world around me darkens.

My gaze snaps to the castle, where I can now vaguely sense her, and my eyes narrow.

Spreading my wings wide, I soar into the sky a moment later, following the faint pull of my connection to Callie. The darkness moves with me, swarming along the edges of the palace grounds and dimming the fae lights until they're nothing more than a memory.

I move to the invisible barrier that bars me entrance into the Fauna palace. While I can't see it, I can sense the ward arcing over the royal grounds in a perfect dome.

Must get to her.

Pulling a fist back, I begin to hammer against the barrier that separates me from the keep.

THWUMP! THWUMP! THWUMP! The sound of my blows pulsates through the night.

It doesn't take long for the Fauna soldiers to react. Between the thick shadows that have curled themselves around the outskirts of the palace and the sonic booms of each successive blow, they know someone's trying to breach their castle.

But cloaked in darkness as I am, they can't see me.

I strike the magical barrier again and again, putting my power into it. Each time I feel the wards give a little more.

THWUMP—THWUMP—THWUMP!

Got to get to her.

THWUMP—THWUMP!

The primal need is stirring me into a frenzy.

Now that I can hear Callie's essence, each note of her call is getting increasingly dire.

I throw all that I've got into the hits, barely aware that my knuckles are splitting and my blood is dripping down the ward and onto the ground.

Finally the guards on duty spot where I'm trying to enter. On the other side of the barrier they run toward me, weapons drawn. The shit thing about wards is that, while things can't pass from my side into theirs, things can move from their side into mine—namely arrows. The soldiers notch them into their bows then let them fly. One—two—three—four whiz by me. More follow, until the night air is filled with the hushed zipping sound of them.

I grunt as an arrow hits me in the shoulder. Another thumps into my side.

Bound to happen with that many soldiers taking aim at me.

I don't slow my ministrations. Beneath my fist I sense the ward growing brittle. I strike it again and again.

With a crack, it finally shatters, the magic rippling across the dome as the ward disintegrates.

I'm in! I almost roar with my feral triumph.

I dissipate into the darkness just as a barrage of arrows shoot past me. Those that were buried in my flesh fall harmlessly to the ground.

In this form it's hard to focus on my connection to Callie; now more than ever our magic is incompatible. But I'm near enough to her to home in on her essence.

I manifest outside Karnon's throne room. This section of the castle grounds is warded once more against me.

Fucker knew I'd be coming for my mate.

Inside, I can hear Callie's screams. It breaks something inside me.

Never borne such agony! It feels like someone is ripping the flesh from my bones.

Karnon did this.

The darkness gathers around me, extinguishing all memory of light.

There's a calmness inside me, a calmness honed by a lifetime of practice. Everything shuts down—my love, my hate, my dreams and fears. All that's left of me is a stillness.

I gather my magic and throw it at the large double doors barring me entrance.

BOOM!

They tremble against my power but hold fast.

Again.

BOOM!

I hear wood and metal creak as it begins to buckle.

Again.

BOOM!

The air in front of me ripples.

Again.

BOOM!

With a shriek, the spell shatters and the doors burst open, the wooden frame splintering and the metal fastenings screeching as they're ripped away from the wall. They sound like thunder as they hit the ground.

Inside the throne room is a nightmarish scene. Dead vines stretch up the walls and ceiling, curving around the throne of bones. Old leaves decorate the ground. The place has fallen into decay.

Amongst it all is Karnon, his eyes wild and frenzied, and at his feet—

I don't immediately process the sight of the crumpled body in the middle of the room. That limp, bloody thing can't be a person.

But then I hear our connection and smell her scent.

My mate.

My *Callie*.

I have to lock my legs to keep from falling. I can't stop the agonized bellow that escapes my throat.

No.

My darkness curls around her protectively.

"So your mate found you after all," Karnon says from where he looms over her. "Took him long enough."

I'm at Callie's side in an instant, and now I am falling to my knees. Her heartbeat is a weak, thready thing. I choke on my own breath as I take it all in. Whatever happened to her, she only barely escaped it.

My hand trembles as it passes over her. So much blood. I'm afraid to touch her.

And then I notice the feathers, the hundreds of bloody, night-dark feathers that sprout from a pair of—of wings. Wings attached to my mate's *back*. And now I do touch her, so I can feel for myself that they're real.

They are. The wet feathers shiver just the slightest beneath my palm.

I turn my hand over and see blood coating my skin. A noise slips from my throat.

"Gods," I whisper, as my gaze moves from my hands to take in Callie's all over again, the horror of what was done to her washing over me. "Is anything...broken?"

A sob works its way out of my mate, and she pinches her eyes shut, as though to block out the reality of the situation.

I thought my heart was already pulverized, but apparently not because I feel it shatter at the sight of my wounded, shaking siren. My hold tightens on her, despite my fear that I might be hurting her.

Around us, my shadows thicken, swarming protectively over my mate.

I feed them a little magic.

...We saw it...

...terrible, terrible sight...

...sprouted clean from her back...

...Fauna King to blame...

I feel my rage then, my sweet, faithful rage, begin to gather.

"I'm so sorry, cherub," I say, my voice cracking. "For everything. He will pay."

"Tell me, how do you like your mate now?" the Fauna King says. "She's improved, no?"

I brush a kiss against Callie's temple. My eyes travel up, to the mad, antlered king.

Gently, I release my siren and stand. The only sign of my thunderous mood are the shadows thickening around me.

"You know it's breaking the most sacred law of hospitality to attack a king within his own castle," Karnon taunts even as he begins to back up.

I move toward him, the darkness nipping at my heels. The long years I've lived with the memory of my mother, broken and lifeless, dead at the hands of another king. And me, powerless to stop it.

"I never imagined you'd go for a slave," Karnon continues. "But weak attracts weak…"

I could not save my mother, and I could not stop this from happening to my mate—but I was always good at vengeance.

My magic is building, building…

Rip. Kill. My instincts scream at me.

"Though I did enjoy her moans…"

Rip—kill.

Karnon lets out a frustrated growl, then in a fit of impatience he flings his magic at me. His phantom claws shred through my clothes and slice into my flesh.

"No," Callie groans weakly.

My magic stitches the wounds up, but even as they're healing, Karnon strikes again. And again. And again.

My clothes tear and my skin is split open. Blood gushes from the wounds, dripping onto the ground. I can't feel the warmth of my blood against my skin or the sharp sting of pain. My senses have dulled as the deep abyss of my magic opens up.

All I can focus on is Karnon.

Rip. Kill.

My power gathers, coiling around me. It feels as if the

universe has lent me its darkness, the shadows slipping in from the world around me. I sense their longing for this powerful king.

Karnon's movements are becoming erratic. More than once I catch sight of the whites of his eyes.

"Your woman tasted good too—have I told you that?" he says, still trying to goad me. "Mortal flesh is so sweet when ripe. But humans, they break so easily. Look at yours—" He gestures to Callie. "Nearly dead from a simple metamorphosis."

I don't bother looking. I don't want to drag my eyes off this marked man who dared to touch my mate.

Rip. Kill.

It's only when my mate's pained voice cries out that I drag my gaze from Karnon. She lays on the ground, the floor smeared a little with her blood. Her entire body trembles with exhaustion.

My power builds, buzzing in my veins. My mother's lifeless face flashes before my eyes. Callie's weak, bloody one stares at me.

Finally, I do feel something. I feel far *too* much.

I am choking on my own love for Callie, and I'm drowning in my own ineptitude that I didn't find her sooner, get here quicker. My soul mate, who has already endured so much at the hands of a bad man, has now been terrorized by another monster.

My attention swings back to Karnon.

Rip. Kill.

My power surges within me, the darkness expanding through the room, snuffing out the lights one by one.

Eviscerate him. Feed him his own bowls. Tear his heart from his chest and force him to look at it so that he might

232

know what it feels like to have that which is most precious to him held in the hands of his enemy.

Karnon must sense my blighted thoughts because he stumbles, even as he continues to slash me with those claws again and again.

Yes, I am something even monsters fear.

They are always frightened in the end, every one of my victims. Not because I'm apathetic or because I enjoy blood sport, but because they realize the one simple truth behind my existence—

I was made to kill.

The Fauna King turns to Callie. I don't realize his foolhardy plan until he is practically upon her. He grabs my mate and hauls her against him. She cries out as her trapped wings are crushed between them.

At the sound of her cry, I draw on my vast darkness, pulling deeply from the night and letting my magic thicken in my veins.

One does not just fuck with my mate and live to see dawn.

The Mad Fauna King wraps a hand around her neck, his claws digging into the soft skin of her neck.

"I will hurt her," Karnon threatens, staring me down.

I go still, the shadows billowing around me.

Rip. Kill.

I lost Callie once. I won't again.

My gaze moves to my mate, and I want her to know: I am not afraid, and she should not be either. *We* are the things of nightmares.

My shadows move like snakes across the floor, spreading my darkness.

I return my attention to Karnon, who must sense his own

end. He glances down as the shadows lick and twine their way up him and Callie. I stare at him even as my shadows swallow up the last vestiges of light. I stare until there is nothing but the primordial void my ancestors crawled out of.

"You think I cannot see in the dark?" the Fauna King says.

I smile, and the void smiles with me.

"I am the dark."

My power blasts out of me, rippling through the room and destroying everything in its path. It vaporizes the Fauna King and the walls of the palace. It blows apart furniture, shatters windows, rips off roofs. Across the palace grounds, any Fauna fae caught in the web of my darkness now burst like overripe fruit as my darkness devours them.

My magic encounters another ward, and it flays the spell wide open, allowing my shadows to rush in. In an instant I become aware of an entire subterranean prison located beneath the palace and the hundreds of women held captive within it. My darkness does its work, shredding through prison guard after prison guard.

The whole thing is over in a matter of seconds.

I bow my head as my power sweeps back into me. The only ones to survive the ordeal are Callie and the captive women. Everyone else has disintegrated into magic and dust.

I lift my head, my gaze finding that of my bloody mate. "The King of Fauna is no more."

CHAPTER 25
THE FUTURE IS NOW

Present

The hour is late, but here in the Night Kingdom, it makes no difference. The sky is just as dark as it always is, and the stars twinkle just as brightly as they always do.

I lie in my royal chambers, my mate at my side.

I stare down at Callie, her dark hair fanned out around her, her eyes closed and her lips parted in sleep. A soft sigh escapes her.

It's almost unbearable, caring this much for someone else. I have half a mind to wake Callie up, just so I can slide into her and feel her around me.

I settle for tracing one rounded earlobe.

Never have I been so thankful to see my mate safe in my bed.

...not true...

...you're always thanking the bloody night that she's in your bed...

My lips quirk, before the expression dissolves away into something more somber.

Almost lost her.

Even now I can acutely remember the sight of her in the Flora Queen's sacred oak forest, her essence slipping further and further away from me as she bled out from a knife wound inflicted by the Thief of Souls. For several horrible seconds, I had to grapple with the possibility that my mate was gone.

If I hadn't fed her the lilac wine…

Even now a small shudder works through me. *Unendurable*. And to think of how many centuries I have left to live. It's impossible to imagine spending them alone.

My thumb brushes her lower lip, causing her to murmur in her sleep.

Now I won't have to.

I've taken her, I've claimed her, and now I get to keep her. She's tasted lilac wine, and the elixir has both given her everlasting life and made two magics that were once incompatible, compatible. The cord that binds us pulls on my heartstrings even now, and through it I can hear the dark, alluring notes of Callie's power, her siren calling to me.

A noise on the balcony has me out of bed in an instant. I slip on a shirt and pants and head to the doors that lead out, my wings flaring behind me. Wings that, not so long ago, my father had broken. They've healed, but the memory hasn't.

I step onto the balcony, which is completely deserted— just as it should be—and I lean against the railing.

Galleghar Nyx, the Shadow King, is still out there. What a fool I'd been all those years ago to not question why his body had been impervious to the elements. I'd been so filled with hate for him that I let it cloud my judgment. It's clear to me now that Galleghar was kept in a state somewhere between life and death—much like the sleeping women. And there's little doubt in my mind who was responsible for my father's unnatural stupor. At some point in time, Galleghar must've tied his fate and his allegiance to that of the Thief.

And now the Otherworld is paying the price for it.

I stand outside a few minutes longer, taking in the pale buildings that spread out around me.

An unnatural sort of silence descends upon Somnia. The back of my neck pricks.

...*He...Is...Here...*

I turn around, my shadows billowing out of me as I head back inside.

Who?

....

I stride into the bedroom, and that's when I see it.

A shadow looms over Callie, one dark arm reaching out to pet her hair.

Kill. The thought is instinctual.

My darkness unleashes itself. It sweeps across the room, wrapping around the shadow. I expect my magic to devour the creature, as it does all magical things, but it won't.

It...*can't.*

The thing cackles once, a wispy, hollow sound that seems to come from somewhere else, and then it's gone.

I only get moments to make sense of what I saw. Then the quiet night is quiet no longer.

A thousand screams shatter the silence. They come from deep in the bowels of the castle, the shrieks shaking the earth.

I know what I'm hearing before even the shadows can confirm it.

The sleeping women in the caskets have awoken.

Keep a lookout for the final book in
Laura Thalassa's The Bargainer series

Dark Harmony

CHAPTER 1

I stare down at my hands for the fiftieth time since Des and I returned from the Flora Kingdom, looking for something that indicates I'm different. *Changed.*

Immortal.

I press my palm to my heart. Beneath the steady thump of it, I feel something else. Something magical and mysterious.

Something that wasn't there just days ago.

My connection to Des thrums under my touch like a second heartbeat, the two of us now magically bound together.

I slide him a coy glance.

Des sits along a thick stone railing, his back resting against one of the columns bolted into the rocky island. The two of us linger on the lowest balcony of Somnia, one of the six floating islands of the Night Kingdom and the capital of the Bargainer's realm.

"I'm angry at you, you know," I say, though there's no venom to the words.

The Bargainer's eyes are closed, his head tipped back against the column. "I know."

I watch him as he sits on the very edge of the world, the dark night beyond him. In the distance, the chittering laughter of pixies rides the evening wind.

"You never asked me if I wanted to live forever." My voice catches on that last word.

Technically, I'm not going to live *forever*, but it might as well be that long. Thanks to the lilac wine Des fed me, I'm now looking at a solid four hundred years of life—if not more.

What will the earth look like by the time I actually kick the bucket? How about the Otherworld?

Need to talk to Temper about how freaking long fairy lifespans are.

The Bargainer's eyes open, his glittering silver gaze looking fearsome and fae.

He gives me a hint of a smile, though there's no humor in it. "Cherub, you seem to be forgetting the fact you were dying at the time."

I was dying, and he was unwilling to let me go.

He reaches out a hand to me, and his magic tugs me toward him. I frown as I'm ushered to his side.

Des taps my mouth. "Tell me, Callie," he says, his voice like honeyed wine as his hands fall to my waist, "don't you want to spend more than just a few decades with me?"

Of course I do. That's beside the point.

I'm upset that I didn't get a chance to decide my fate for myself. And now the future looms endlessly ahead of me.

Des lifts his inked arm into the air. Luminescent blue smoke coalesces from the night, solidifying more and more as it snakes its way to the Bargainer's hand. By the time it reaches his palm, it's a glowing cord. I've seen this stuff before: spun moonlight.

The Bargainer manipulates it in his hand, working the eerie substance until it's not just a cord but an elaborate necklace.

I narrow my eyes as he brings the unearthly jewelry to my throat.

"That's not fair," I say as he clasps it behind my neck, even as my fingertips reach for the necklace. "You can't just pull one of your pretty fairy tricks and buy my forgiveness."

But he can, and he has, and he will do so again. These neat little tricks of his have made me forgive a lot.

The Bargainer turns on his perch so his legs straddle mine. He pulls me in close, my hips fitting snugly between his thighs. "My pretty fairy tricks are what you like best about me," he says, his lips skimming my mouth as he talks. His gaze drops to my lips. "Well, that and my di—"

"*Des*."

He laughs against my skin, his warm breath drawing out my gooseflesh. Slowly, the laughter dies from his features. "I lost you once, Callie," he says, "and those seven years nearly killed me. I don't intend to lose you again."

My gut clenches at the memory. Even now I can feel the ache of his absence; it's a wound that never healed.

Des presses a hand to my heart. "Besides—is this not worth it?"

He doesn't need to elaborate on what *this* is.

Beneath his palm, I feel the warmth of Des's presence—not only against my skin but *within* me. It feels like I'm being kissed by pale moonlight, like the stars and the deep night rest under my skin, and I know that makes no sense, but there it is.

His magic even has a sound. It's a low melody, the faint

notes just beyond my reach. It makes me feel the same breathless excitement I used to feel at Peel Academy when evening was coming and Des was coming with it.

We were once mates separated by worlds and magic; now we're separated no longer, thanks to the lilac wine.

The wine came with other perks. I can now make my claws and scales and wings appear and disappear at will. And I can sense fae magic in a way I never could before.

Of course, there are drawbacks too—fairy gifts *always* have drawbacks.

I'm still coming for you. Your life is mine.

The Bargainer catches my wrist, examining my bare forearm.

"Three hundred and twenty-two favors—a lifetime's worth," he murmurs.

I follow his gaze. It's weird looking down and not seeing the Bargainer's bracelet. The skin there is paler than the rest, and I admit, my arm feels naked without the weight of all those black beads. I wore that bracelet every day for nearly eight years…and overnight it disappeared.

It was a lifetime's worth of beads, but in the end, it was even more than that—it was a *life's* worth. Those beads brought me back from the edge of death. And now I have to wonder if, from the very beginning, Des's magic somehow knew it would come to this. If all that debt and all those years of waiting were its way of gathering magic so it could prevent my untimely death.

Or maybe I just got really, really lucky.

I lower my wrist so I can look the Night King in the eye. "Anger aside—thank you." My words come out rough.

Thank you is a pitifully small show of gratitude for what Des did. Because he saved me. *Again.*

For once I'd like to return the favor.

Des's hand tightens around my forearm, and he brings my wrist to his lips, then presses a kiss there. "Does this mean you forgive me for the lilac wine?"

"Don't push your luck, fairy boy."

"Cherub, hasn't anyone told you? I don't need luck. I deal in favors."

CHAPTER 2

That evening, I stand in what feels like a void, endless darkness pressing in on all sides. I glance about, unsure how I arrived there.

"Not a slave anymore, I see."

My shoulders hike up at that voice.

That *voice.*

Last time I heard it, I was in the Flora Queen's sacred oak forest, my life bleeding out of me. And now it's at my back.

"We meet again, enchantress," the Thief of Souls says.

The monster's fingertips trail like velvet up my arm.

"Your wings are gone—" He leans forward and breathes me in. "And is that fae magic I smell? Could it be that the mighty Night King gave you the lilac wine?"

"Don't act like you're surprised," I say.

The Thief had deliberately orchestrated a situation where I'd drink the wine and become fae, all so that his power could be compatible with mine. Before then, his magic didn't work on me, just as it didn't for all humans.

"What can I say?" he responds. "Fairies in love can be terribly predictable, I'm afraid."

The Thief comes around to my front, and I finally get a good look at him.

He's as I remember him from my dreams and that moment in the woods. Jet-black hair, upturned inky eyes, pouty mouth, alabaster skin.

Like all the other fairies I've met, he's beautiful. Almost unbearably so. Not for the first time, I wish evil looked as it should.

I step away from his touch. The night shrouds us on all sides, but even in the darkness, I can make out the twisted oaks that surround me.

My stomach drops. I'm back in Mara Verdana's sacred oak forest.

Could've sworn I'd left this place.

Off in the distance, I hear the faint notes of a fiddle and the snap and crackle of a bonfire. The smell of woodsmoke carries on the breeze. There's something under the smell, a scent that's somewhat sweet. If only I could place it…

The Thief of Souls walks over to a tree, and his boot scuffs a root. "This, I believe, is where you fucked the Night King."

Bile rises into my throat.

Jesus. Had he watched us?

His gaze meets mine. "How do I know that?" He glances at the tree trunk again. The normally rough bark is coated in a slick substance. "I have eyes everywhere."

As I watch, the Thief presses a hand to the glistening bark. Within seconds, whatever coats the tree trunk now spills onto the Thief's hand, the dark rivulets snaking between his fingers and down his wrist.

And now I place that strange scent.

Blood.

It drips from the tree the Thief touches, and now it's smeared across his hand.

He gives me a small smile, his eyes glinting in the darkness.

I hear the slow patter of rain. Only I'm not sure it's *rain* dripping from the trees' boughs.

As I watch, the oak in front of me starts to groan and tremble.

The Thief eyes me up and down. "Fae magic suits you well, enchantress. I confess I'm eager to see how it interacts with my own."

Around me, the trees crack and splinter, making wet popping noises.

One by one, the trunks peel open like banana skins. Nestled inside each is a sleeping soldier, all of them still as death. Blood oozes down their skin and drips from their tattered clothes.

The oak next to the Thief ruptures, revealing a bronze-skinned fairy. The Thief touches the soldier's cheek, and for an instant, his face morphs into that of the sleeping man. Then the illusion is gone, and the Thief is himself once more.

I shudder.

"I've been waiting a while for this day to come," he says distractedly, still staring at the soldier. He drops his hand from the sleeping man and turns his full attention to me. "Tell me, enchantress, can you make a man—any man—fall in love with you? Not just enchant them for a time but truly conquer their hearts?"

My skin prickles.

The Thief leaves the soldier's side, pacing toward me. Around us, the sound of wood splintering and blood dripping swells until I feel I might go mad.

All at once, the woods fall eerily silent.

Without warning, my siren flares to life, triggered by some pressing, unknown fear. My skin brightens, illuminating the Thief's face in the dark night.

His eyes take on a fascinated sheen. "*Yes,*" he says, almost to himself, "I bet you could." He closes the distance between us. "I do miss the days when I thought you a simple slave. Perhaps when you are mine, I'll pretend you still are one." He catches one of my wrists. "You'll wear metal cuffs and a collar like the slaves of old. And then you'll be my *enslaved* enchantress, and together we'll see just how close you can come to making someone like me feel affection."

He dares to threaten us? Never again will we fall under anyone's yoke.

"I hope you can manage it," he continues, "more for your sake than mine. I'm not known for being gentle with my playthings. Just ask Mara."

I stare at him for a long moment, my claws sharpening, barely staying my siren's violent tendencies. Then, all at once, I release my hold on her.

My free hand moves almost without me noticing it. I strike, swiping at his face. My claw tips tear open the skin of his cheek in four evenly spaced lines.

Almost immediately, blood begins to drip from the wounds.

The Thief looks amused.

I don't get any warning before he throws me against the tree he'd been toeing only minutes before.

I let out an angry shout as I hit the bloody trunk, my

chest pressed against the sleeping soldier, my eyes staring at the man's bloody face. Behind me, the Thief pins me in.

"Normally, I like my women docile," he whispers against my ear, "but you—you, I'll enjoy fighting. Breaking."

His words are decidedly sexual, and I remember all those female soldiers and the children he'd forced upon them.

I grit my teeth, my nails digging into the tree trunk.

Never, my siren vows. *We will kill him first, and we will relish it.*

I hear a moan on the wind, and the trees shiver, their leaves falling from the branches like tears.

In front of me, the soldier's eyes snap open.

Oh *shit.*

The Thief leans into my ear again, his lips brushing the sensitive skin there. "Enjoy the carnage. I do hope you survive it…"

———

Screams rip me from sleep.

I jerk up in bed, wide awake in an instant, my breath coming in startled gasps.

Not in the queen's oak forest. Not pinned to a rotting tree.

Not in the Thief's clutches.

The dim lamps hanging above me illuminate the Bargainer's Otherworld chambers.

I'm safe. For now.

The screams filter back through my awareness.

Then again…

Des stands at the foot of the bed, his talon-tipped wings spread, looking like one of hell's angels as he stares at a point above my head. I follow his gaze, but there's nothing there.

My eyes meet his as more shrieks vibrate through the

bones of the castle. There's something about the sound… like it's one voice coming through many mouths.

I remember my dream, the soldier's eyes opening. Something cold skitters up my spine.

There are no sleeping men here in the Night Kingdom, I try to reassure myself. And it's true, there are no sleeping men here in Somnia. But a thousand feet beneath us, an army's worth of women lie sleeping.

The screams seem to get louder.

At least, the women *were* sleeping.

I'm pretty goddamn sure they're awake now.

About the Author

Found in the forest when she was young, Laura Thalassa was raised by fairies, kidnapped by werewolves, and given over to vampires as repayment for a hundred-year-old debt. She's been brought back to life twice, and with a single kiss, she woke her true love from eternal sleep. She now lives happily ever after with her undead prince in a castle in the woods.

…or something like that anyway.

When not writing, Laura can be found scarfing down guacamole, hoarding chocolate for the apocalypse, or curled up on the couch with a good book.

You can find more news and updates on Laura Thalassa's books at http://laurathalassa.com.